The Blacksmith Legacy

The Blacksmith Legacy

SCÉAL AR CHLÁNN

November 2007

Dear Marcus,

Wishing you sunny days and Good Fortunes!

Margaret Finn Hochberg, Ed.D.

Margaret Finn Hochberg

To order additional copies of this book, contact:
Xlibris Corporation
1-888-795-4274
www.Xlibris.com
Orders@Xlibris.com
17560

Today there is a new Ireland emerging.
It is a nation that has grown a century in a matter of years. It is
prosperous and expanding.
Its young people no longer need to leave;
no longer need to experience the heartaches
of separation.
Today, the experiences of the young in our family will be different.
Different from those who have come before in Ireland, different from
those who have come before in America. It is for the young of both
countries that this is written,
that they may better understand
and value the lives that paved the way.

Introduction

SINCE I WAS a child, when family and Irish friends would gather, there would be stories of "home." I would listen with rapt attention to strange sounding names and songs like Galway Bay and the Green Glens of Antrim.

I was sixteen the first time I visited Ireland. My grandparents had already passed, but I visited their home places, walked their lanes and for the first time, began to understand the Ireland I had seen through my parents' eyes.

My need to know only increased with this experience. I wondered how my grandparents survived the loss of their children. My father's parents lost all four children, not to disease, but to emigration. In one melancholy letter Grandmother wrote, "all my little birds have flown the nest." She wondered if the pain of leaving was greatest for those remaining.

It has taken twelve years to compile the family genealogy, collect the stories and write this book. In many symbolic ways, it is for me, an end to the searching. My family has been found.

"To be ignorant of what occurred
before you were born
is to remain always a child.
For what is the worth of human life,
Unless it is woven into the life
Of our ancestors by the records of time."

-Cicero

PART I

THE EARLY DAYS

Clareboy, Co.Cavan
1885

THE IRON HAMMER hit the anvil with a loud clang. The horseshoe was ready for fitting. The horse nearby whinnied and pulled at the earth with her bare hoof, as if impatient with the wait. The farmer holding the horse reins tightened his grip and made ready for the smithy.

Patrick Lynch, the blacksmith, had to squint his eyes as he stepped out of the dimness of the fire-lit forge into the bright sunlight of afternoon. With practiced moves he turned his back to the horse's tail, lifted the back hoof between his two legs and fitted the horseshoe to the exposed sole. He pulled a sharp file from his apron pocket and worked in quick short strokes to customize the fit. One at a time, he took the half dozen spike nails from between his lips, and skillfully attached the horseshoe. In a few moments he was finished and patting the old mare on her rump.

"That's a fine job you've done," said the grateful farmer as he handed Paddy a shilling.

"Ah, 'tis a good working day all right and please God, if needed, we'll be here 'til the sun goes down," answered Paddy, wiping his sweat-covered forehead with the sleeve of his shirt.

It was springtime in Clareboy and there was much work to be done in the fields. Every farmer needed his horses in good working condition to get the fields prepared and the planting done. Every daylight hour a farmer waited at the forge was an hour less in his fields. This day there had been four farmers waiting for Paddy when he opened the forge at dawn. The men knew that waiting half a day for Paddy was worth getting the job done right and some had traveled as far as eight miles.

Paddy's arms were muscular and strong from the daily work of the forge and he swung his hammer with graceful ease. Watching his wide, strong swing was like watching an athlete at the peak of his performance. He stoked the fire and handled the bellows the way he handled himself. He was reliable, determined and resourceful. Born in 1843, his childhood had been a struggle for survival during the years of The Great Famine. But he had done more than survive, he had thrived.

Paddy's life had been content until one fateful day when he traveled to town. He spied a cluster of people chatting and laughing on the footpath. Recognizing neighbors, he approached the group to discover the source of excitement. In the middle stood Rose Morgan, a friend from his schooldays. She had returned from a stay in Dublin wearing a city dress, a hat from one of the finest shops, a new air of confidence and a wonderful smile. This Rose was a new creature; someone he had never laid eyes on before. She spotted him, called his name and extended her hand.

Since that morning, the daylight hours were too long. Paddy was hurrying through his daily chores at the forge in anticipation of evening. He would close the forge, change his clothing and cut across the fields to visit Rose at the Morgan cottage.

Rose was always delighted to see Paddy coming and after

several weeks, if the weather was fine, she sat outside waiting for him to arrive. Paddy could not believe how quickly she had become so important to him. He had never experienced such an attraction before and he wondered how he had survived before he found her. On Saturday nights and Sunday afternoons, they walked to the crossroads together to join in the music and dancing. The following spring, Bridget "Rose" Morgan and Patrick Lynch announced their engagement and married in Drumkilly Chapel. Rose joined Paddy in his cottage next to the forge.

The cottage was similar to that of Paddy's neighbors with two rooms; a window in each and a cottage half-door. The half door allowed the sunlight in during the day while keeping the assortment of hens and chicks outside in the yard. The focal point of the main room was the huge hearth built to create the wall between the two rooms. Fueled with turf cut from the local bog, it kept the household warm and provided heat for cooking and baking. The hearth dried wet clothing when the sunshine failed and gave the entire room a golden glow of welcome.

A black pot for boiling water hung on the iron swinger along with one for porridge and a stewpot. The furniture was simple, sturdy and functional. There was a butter churn to the side of the hearth and a spinning wheel stood in the corner.

According to family legend, the spinning wheel was nearly one hundred years old. In 1790, farmers were encouraged by the British to grow flax. For every acre planted with flax, the farmer received a spinning wheel. Laurence Lynch, blacksmith and farmer in this same forge and on this same land one hundred years earlier, agreed to plant an acre of flax to obtain the spinning wheel. His two daughters became spinners.

When Rose moved into the cottage, she began to add her favorite colors to the two rooms. In just a short time, it was a cozy home with a baby on the way. A son was born in 1887. They named him John.

Each day was a busy one. There were eggs to collect with hens, chickens and a donkey to feed. Paddy milked their one

cow twice a day and Rose skimmed the cream to churn some
butter. She mixed the ingredients for brown bread, placed it
in a round black pot with a cover and set it to bake at the
bottom of the hearth with turf stacked around to even the
heat. Paddy could smell the bread baking while he worked in
the forge and he smiled at the thought of his wonderful life.

Rose and the baby would visit the forge frequently bringing
tea or lunch to Paddy and sometimes chatting about the latest
news with the waiting neighbor men. Behind the cottages were
the two Lynch fields and Rose's vegetable garden. She grew
potatoes, carrots, turnips and, when the rabbits allowed, lettuce.
While the baby took his morning nap, Rose weeded and tended
to the vegetables. She picked berries in season, made apple
tart and apple sauce from the fruit tree and canned the extra.
At the end of the day with the chores completed, Paddy and
Rose would share the warmth of a fire and delight in being
together with little Johnny.

In October, Rose was pregnant with their second child.
She was pleased that the baby was due in June, before the
summer heat. She believed that July and August would give
her time to rest. By fall, she would be strong enough to help
Paddy bring in the hay. Rose's vegetable garden was going well
and combined with the forge, there would be a little extra for
the coming winter and another mouth to feed. Rose was happy
in her new role as wife and mother.

Rose's second son arrived early on the morning of June 4,
1888. There was no discussion about his name. He was Patrick
after his father, as John had been named after his grandfather.
It was the Irish tradition and it would be honored. At fifteen
months of age, Johnny was now the oldest son of the family.

The baby was thriving but Rose was tired. The summer heat
and the labor of bearing her second son had taken a toll. The
month of June came and went. July brought unusual heat and
the farmers' fields began to scorch under the summer sun.
Rose was ill with a fever. The doctor prescribed lots of broth,

cold compresses for the fever and continued rest. Rose complied and Paddy closed the forge to help in the cottage with Johnny and the baby. He made fresh broth each morning. He faithfully went to the well for cold spring water every hour. He gently wrapped Rose in the cooling cloth, all the while speaking words of comfort and encouragement to her.

August came but it brought little improvement for Rose. Kathleen, a friend and neighbor, offered to stay with Rose and the children so Paddy could gather the hay. Grateful for the offer, Paddy set out to work in his fields. As he pitched the dry hay into stacks, his mind began to wander. Suddenly, the thought crashed on top of him, toppling his balance and making him unsteady. Like a wave building up slowly, then crashing on the seashore, the realization struck him. Rose was dying. He felt it with his whole being. Why Rose? Why now? He dropped his pitchfork and ran from the field to stay at Rose's bedside.

Three of the neighbors stopped in to see Rose on Sunday morning and the parish priest came by after Mass. When everyone had left, Rose asked Patrick to bring the two boys to her. He did as she asked, and with a mother's love, she kissed her babies goodbye. She told Paddy that she was going to die but he would have none of it. He whispered words of love to her, told her how much he needed her, the boys needed her and that she would beat this fever, be strong again and plant more flowers next spring. That evening, August 26, 1888, Rose died quietly with her young family beside her in the cottage she loved so well.

September 1888

After Rose's funeral, Paddy was distraught and for the first time in his life, he felt trapped and powerless. His strength was gone and his grief turned to anger. He was angry with a God who would take his Rose. He stumbled around the cottage and yard without purpose.

Jim Galligan, a good friend, visited everyday. Jim made certain the baby was getting milk and fed porridge to Johnny.

"Paddy, pull yourself together man. You must take care of yourself. Get the forge up and running. The men will begin to go elsewhere if you don't reopen." He paused before continuing, letting the words settle on Paddy. Paddy bowed his head.

Jim began to pace in a circle around the small area before the hearth. He was pleading his case as if he were in the High Court. When Paddy looked up and made eye contact, Jim continued in a pleading voice.

"How will you take care of business with an infant in the house? The baby must go to someone. Are you listening to me, man?" Jim's voice rose louder.

"The baby must go. The sooner, the better. Promise me." Paddy nodded.

Paddy knew that his friend was right, but he was not settled. His anger interfered with his thinking and he was having difficulty quieting the voice inside that told him to keep the boys together. He was sure that Rose would want him to do that. At night he would check the sleeping boys and wonder at their gentle faces and their dependency on him. Somehow, their weakness renewed his strength. He would build his family strong.

Three weeks after Rose's funeral, on a cloudy morning in September, the strong blacksmith hands gently wrapped baby Patrick in a blanket. Paddy delivered his three-month-old son to the care of Teresa O'Malley, a midwife in Cavan Town.

Twenty Years Later
January 1908

Amongst the neighbors, the Lynch cottage had a reputation as the "bachelor house." Patrick and Johnny were now good looking men in their twenties living with their father. Over the years, the three men had fallen into a comfortable routine.

Young Patrick had taken on the responsibility of the farm. He loved the fields and took great pride in having the best milk production around the area. He would rise early each day, milk the cows, load the cart with the large tins, hitch the horse and head for the creamery. Once there, the men would line up the carts in the lane while the inspectors checked the milk quality and weighed the volume. The farmers used the time to grab a smoke and catch up on the conversation about town or the latest hurling score.

Johnny, the older of the two brothers, had been in the forge since he was a teenager, so it seemed only natural that he now continued to work side by side with his father.

Johnny had a talent for football. He joined the Crosserlough Gaels and played in every Sunday match. If the bruises were not too many, he would be back again on a weeknight for practice.

Patrick was the opposite of Johnny when it came to sports. He never played yet he never missed a chance to yell support from the sidelines. The brothers would cycle to the matches, sometimes ten or fifteen miles. Patrick loved the cycling. He and Johnny would have great chats along the way. The chat was about this and that, sometimes girls and sometimes the future.

"You can't be always worrying about the future," Johnny would say to his brother.

"Sure I'm not worrying. I'm just trying to make some plans. If you don't have a plan, Johnny, you'll never get anywhere," would be Patrick's reply.

"Life isn't like that, Patrick. Life happens. You just go out and play it for all its worth. Like the football match. Sometimes you'll win and sometimes you won't. There's no telling what the opposition will be that day."

"Aye, no telling what the opposition will be but maybe, just maybe, you should choose not to play at all that day—and look how different things could turn out."

"What do you mean, not play?" asked John.

"I don't know what I mean exactly, just that you can't always just let things happen to you, sometimes you have to plan to make them happen," answered Patrick.

The two brothers would go back and forth until one would be silent or the destination was reached.

If father was not in the forge, he would meet up with the lads and the men from the village. They would wager on the outcome of the game or bet a pint on how many goals one player could score. Da was proud of John's prowess on the football field and just as proud of Patrick's quick mind. He believed Rose would be pleased with her two sons.

Spring 1909

Johnny's football uniform was in shreds. He had repaired it as best he could but his large blacksmith hands had difficulty with the smallness of a sewing needle. As he sat trying to repair the jersey for the third time, his brother Patrick had a suggestion.

"Why don't you take that jersey to the Keogh cottage? I hear one of the daughters has a sewing machine."

"Aye, the machine stitching would hold much better," added his father.

"It will cost you half a shilling, but if it will get another season, it's worth it."

The Keogh farmhouse was only two fields behind the Lynch forge and cottage. The Keoghs were a large family with seven children and both parents, compared to the small Lynch family of three. The two oldest boys, Daniel and Patrick were working in Glasgow, Scotland. The large glassworks in that city had been attracting the young Irish lads with high wages.

Bridget Keogh had made the journey to Glasgow to join her brothers. Unlike the men, Bridget did not find opportunity waiting for her. She was working as a seamstress and the pay was low with little left at the end of the week. She lived in a boarding house with a dozen other women where conditions were crowded. The glasswork refineries that attracted the men spewed a constant cloud of soot into the air. When it rained, the dampness mixed with the soot on the ground and made the pavement a slippery mass of mud. For the women in long dresses, it was a laundry nightmare.

Bridget Keogh Lynch
Glascow, Scotland, circa 1906

Back in Cavan, Bridget's parents were heartsick for her.

"Do you think she'll ever come home again?" Bridget's mother lamented to her husband.

"Margaret, I was thinking just the other day," he said. "If we have a good harvest, we could buy that sewing machine we saw in Cavan Town and Bridget could take in sewing here. If it went well, sure I could build a shop onto our cottage."

"Oh, John! 'Tis a wonderful plan. I'll write to Bridget this very evening."

The harvest was good that fall and Bridget came back to Clareboy in April. One of her first customers was Johnny Lynch, with his football jersey.

Bridget didn't know Johnny when she was growing up. She was five years his senior so they were not pals in school. Her father and brothers had been to the forge numerous times, but never Bridget.

She could put a name on him, if asked, but nothing more. The day he arrived with the football jersey she thought he had a warm smile. After he left, she examined the shirt and the childlike stitching of previous repairs. She became curious.

"Mam, who lives in the Lynch cottage these days?"

"Sure, the three bachelors, as always."

"That solves the mystery then. This shirt looks as if a child has repaired it!"

"Let me see" said Mam. The two women chuckled at the shirt.

"Tis a good thing this shirt found its way to you, Bridget. A little longer and it would have walked to the trash bin itself."

"I really don't know the three bachelors, Mam. Tell me about them."

Mam started the story with Rose. "A lovely creature. She had soft eyes, with a thoughtful look. A real beauty and she would help anyone. She died a few months after having her second baby. It was a terror of a summer. Heat so hot you could cook an egg on a stone. I remember clearly because your father lost ten head of sheep that summer. We tried to keep the sheep cool in the shed and carried water to them but it was no use. Rose was sick around the same time. Poor Paddy Lynch. He was beside himself with grief when he lost her. I thought he would jump into the grave himself if the men weren't holding him. It was so sad with the two boys just babies. That blacksmith worked hard to build a life for the three of them. When Patrick was old enough for school, he brought him home from the midwife and that's the way it's been since, the three men in the cottage. Sure your brothers played football with Johnny before they headed out to Glasgow. I am surprised you don't remember Johnny and Patrick from those days. They are always together at the matches. Patrick is the quiet one. He has Rose's sweetness and wonderful complexion. But what a pair of ears, they do stick out!" Again, the women laughed.

"Why are you asking me this today?" questioned Mam.

"Just wondered why there wasn't a woman in that cottage," replied Bridget.

The following week when Johnny picked up the football shirt, Bridget asked him about his team. He told her more than she ever wanted to know about football. At the end of the conversation, he invited her to the Sunday match. Caught by surprise and unable to think of an excuse quickly, she accepted the invitation.

Months later, when Johnny Lynch asked John Keogh for Bridget's hand in marriage, there was great jubilation in both households. Both fathers approved of the match but Margaret Keogh had some concerns. She took her daughter aside.

"You truly love Johnny?"

"Aye, Mam. I do."

"You know I think the world of him. He will be a good provider for the future. But I worry about you taking on too much. Sure 'twill be like marrying the three of them. You will be doing the cooking and the washing for the cottage. Have you thought it all through child?"

"Aye, me and Johnny spoke of it earlier. His father felt the same as you and told me he's been cooking and washing and looking after himself for years. He and Patrick will continue to handle their own. I will make the noon dinner for all of us. And really, what does it matter? A few more spuds in the pot? Patrick will do the washing up as he always has and his father will contribute to the cost of any items needed from the shop."

"It surely has been thought out!" replied Mam with surprise, relief and pleasure.

Bridget continued. "Aye. I believe Johnny's father was fearful no woman would ever look at his sons for that very reason."

"You are sure about this girl? I don't want you to be resenting the situation in a few years."

"Aye, Mam. Don't be worrying. Everything will be fine, you'll see."

September 1909

Keeping with the Irish custom, when they married, Bridget would live on Johnny's farm. In anticipation, the Lynch cottage was a beehive of activity and based on the amount of excitement, you would think the three men were getting married!

Paddy whitewashed the cottage inside and out. He cleared the walkway around the well. He worked in the forge and created three rings for a new rainwater barrel. He cut the old barrel in half, filled it with soil and planted flowers under the two cottage windows. He whistled as he worked and realized it had been a long time since he had taken an interest in how the place looked. He smiled when he thought of Rose and how she had loved this place. This cottage had been too long without a woman's soft touch.

Patrick also helped. He lowered the height of the iron

swingarm in the hearth. He painted the cottage double door and made some new candles. Outside, he built a fence to keep the chickens from the front yard.

Johnny set to work at the anvil. He made a horseshoe, symbol of good luck and hung it over the cottage door. He created an iron bed frame, just the right length for the room and wide enough for their comfort. He spent a week adding a new thatched roof. The cottage and its surrounding yard were transformed.

The Keogh farmhouse was also humming. Bridget fashioned her wedding gown after one she had seen in a Glasgow shop. She made a crown from ribbon and attached a fingertip length veil. She made a new dress for her mother and her father borrowed a bow tie and top hat for the occasion.

The wedding took place on Monday, November 22, 1909 in the Drumkilly Chapel. The Keogh brothers and sisters attended except for John, who was in America. Many neighbors attended; the Ennis family and the Lynch's from down the lane, plus Bridget's godparents, James McCabe and Bridget Halton. The witnesses for the marriage were Bernie Ennis and the bride's mother. The Keogh's provided the celebration and a wedding cake at their home. It was a splendid day.

Later that night, in the silence of his bed, Johnny's father thought about how different life would have been if Rose had not died so young. Rose would have loved Bridget. In many ways, they were alike. Both were soft spoken with opinions, strength, and enough love for twenty children. He closed his eyes and prayed for the blessings of long life for his son and his bride. "Keep them safe, dear Jesus, they need each other."

The newlyweds worked hard alongside Johnny's father and brother. The four of them ran the farm and forge.

Bridget presented Johnny with their first child, a son, on Valentine's Day, February 14, 1911. As expected, he was christened Patrick, after his grandfather. There was laughter over the confusion that a third Patrick would create. There were only five people in the cottage and three of them were named Patrick! They decided that grandfather should remain Paddy, his son Patrick would be Pat and the new grandson would be "P", although they usually forgot and called the baby, "wee Patrick."

Both sides of the family were delighted with the first grandchild. Bridget's parents, living just across the fields, visited frequently. It was about the time that wee Patrick was learning to sit up that Pat made his announcement. He surprised everyone at the noon dinner.

"I think it's time I be on me own. I've given it a great deal of thought. I've saved some money and tomorrow when I go to town, I'll stop at the office and book a train to Galway. My friend's brother has an opening in a shoe shop and said he'll give me a start. It's time I was on me own."

Johnny put down his fork. "Are you not happy here with us, Pat? Are we pushing you out?"

"Not at all," replied Pat. "I just think 'tis the right time."

His father spoke next. "You must know that we'd rather you stay, but speaking for meself, I can understand. You must know we will miss you."

Bridget looked from Johnny to Pat to his father. It had never occurred to her that Pat would want to leave but once it was spoken, it was obvious. For the first time, she realized that it must be a lonely existence for Pat, while the rest of them were so involved with their new life. Pat was right. She could see it clearly. Time for him to want his own adventure, maybe a wife and his own baby. She spoke with understanding.

"Pat, Galway sounds like a wonderful idea. But don't you ever forget we are your family. This is your home and your land, too. I think I'm going to cry."

There was a huge send-off party for Pat. His father found

it hard to believe it was really happening. It had been too fast for him. At sixty-eight years of age, Paddy was beginning to like things just the way they were. He remembered the pain of separation when Pat was sent to the midwife as a baby and the memory of that pain came flooding back to his consciousness. He thought about his struggles over the years to keep the family together. Now, he was losing Pat again.

City of Galway
November 1911

Pat enjoyed the sights and sounds of Galway. He got his first glimpse of the ocean, just beyond Galway Bay.

He found his friend's brother easily enough and within two days he was working steady at the shoe shop. The customers were plentiful and the style was grand. It was a far cry from the little lane leading to the forge and cottage in Clareboy. Pat found himself excited by the new experiences. He enjoyed discussing world events with the travelers who frequented the shop. They filled his head with stories of a world beyond the Irish shores.

He made new friends and together they would walk the streets of the city every Sunday. They learned where to get the best value for a meal and which pub had the best music. Before six months passed, Galway couldn't hold Pat any longer. He was a man obsessed with seeing the world for himself. All the stories had stirred a passion. One Friday morning, he wrote a hasty letter to father and Johnny, bought a steamship ticket for New York and sailed three days later. It was November, 1911.

As the tender pulled away from the dock and headed towards the ship at anchor in the outer harbor, Pat kept his eyes focused forward. "Don't look backwards," he whispered to himself. "Look to the future." He had no idea what awaited.

The Great War
1914-1918

The war had been raging in Europe for almost three years before the United States of America declared war on Germany and joined the fight, April 6, 1917. The United States had a regular army of only one hundred and twenty-eight thousand men. A call went out for volunteers and a draft was instituted for able-bodied men ages eighteen to forty-five. The total of fighting men and women swelled to five million. Pat Lynch was drafted into the American Expeditionary Forces under the command of General John J. Pershing. They were deployed to France and as Pat's troop carrier passed within two hundred miles of the Irish coast, he never felt further away from home. Soldier was not what he had in mind when he sailed from Galway Bay.

Conditions in France were worse than anything Pat could have imagined. When his troop ship arrived, the beaches and fields were already littered with broken, mangled bodies. His senses were assaulted. There was the stench of decaying flesh, the visual horror and the crying sounds of those unfortunates still alive. Pat did his job in a stupor. He tried to block what he saw, what he heard, what he felt. He got used to living in the trenches with rain and fear and filth. He got used to marching for miles, then digging more trenches for protection. They went to sleep, got up, did it again. Combat was a part of life. The men went for weeks without taking off their boots; afraid the fragile skin would bleed profusely. They ate from cold ration cans and stole cigarettes from the dead. They helped each other and buried each other.

Pat's platoon was still in France when the peace was signed on November 11, 1918. Seven years had passed since he sailed from Galway Bay. He began to think of Christmas and his family in the Clareboy cottage. He sat in the cramped army quarters and wrote to his father.

Patrick Lynch
United States Army, 1918

Clareboy Cottage
Christmas 1918

The weather was mild in Ireland that winter. The rain had been slight and the temperature, while cold, was tolerable. The hay was gathered early and the crops had been plentiful.

Bridget and Johnny were at the cottage with Grandfather Paddy, now 75 years. The two men had traded roles. Johnny was the blacksmith and his father took the role of helper. Everyday Grandfather would rise early and get the forge fire started for Johnny. They each had their own space in the forge and although the talking was sparse, the men enjoyed each other's company.

The family had grown in eight years of marriage. With four children, the cottage was a busy one. Little Patrick was almost seven; then came Mary called "Mollie", age six; followed by Bridget, three years and John aged two. Mary and John were named after the Keogh grandparents and Bridget after her mother. With four children and three adults, the cottage was a busy home.

One weekday morning, the mailman arrived by bicycle. No one saw him pedal down the lane. He caught them by surprise when he called out in a loud voice.

"Letter from France, from the military!"

Suddenly, seven heads appeared from all different directions.

Bridget called to Johnny and his father in the forge. "Come quickly, a letter, a letter from France. Oh, thank God, it is a letter. That means he is alive!"

Johnny accepted the letter from the mailman and read the envelope. "It's for you, Father."

"Sure, me eyes are failing, read it to me. Good and loud so we all can hear the news. I hope he's not writing from a hospital."

"No, 'tis a military address." A hush fell over the little group and Johnny began to read the letter in a clear voice.

5 December 1918

Dear Father,

I wrote you some time ago but I don't know if you ever received it as I have never had a reply, but I do hope that you got it, and that it found you all in good health, as I am first class myself.

Of course you know that I am in the U.S. Army and in France at the present time and had been here when I wrote you last. And now, when the war is over, and I safe and sound, I hope to soon return to the U.S. and probably pay you a visit next summer. I suppose you were all glad to see the war over, as I know it hit you all pretty hard, but now that it is over, we will get paid back.

I wonder if Johnny is just the same as ever and still working away at the anvil?

Well, dear father, this is all now only to send best love to you, Johnny, wife and family. Also, best wishes and card for a Happy Christmas. Tell Johnny to write to both addresses below, as I don't know how long I will be here. So good bye.

From Pat.

P. Lynch	Private Patrick Lynch
c/o Cronin	Base 8, APO 701
321 East 66th Street	American Expeditionary Force
New York, NY	FRANCE

New York City
1919

Pat Lynch was one of the lucky ones. He returned safely from the war. When his division arrived at Fort Dix in New Jersey, all foreign-born men were eligible for United States citizenship. On January 31, 1919, Patrick Lynch, farmer and soldier from Clareboy, County Cavan, recited the oath of allegiance and became the first member of his family to become a citizen of the United States of America. The following day Pat loaded his duffel bag with his belongings, bid farewell to his army buddies and rode the train back to New York City to pick up the pieces of his life.

The city had grown tremendously while he was in France. Returning soldiers and sailors poured into the city. Each one met with open arms as the communities rejoiced at life returning to normal. Pat got together with all his old friends. He found the Cronin brothers, Paddy Galligan from home and the McGibneys. Even one of the Ennis boys from the lane turned up at a football match. They were all together to celebrate Pat's thirty-first birthday in New York.

Finding a job was difficult. After weeks of disappointment, he answered an advertisement for workers in the U.S. Post Office. His new citizenship and military experience gave him the edge over other applicants and he got the position.

War had changed this man. The experiences of battle had lessened his sense of adventure, made him more respectful of each new day. Eating rations from a can made him appreciate a fine meal and the comfort found sitting in an easy chair at home. The decisions he made were more cautious, more deliberate. Starting this job, Pat's life began to take a new direction.

Ten months later Pat got the news from home. Johnny and Bridget wrote that father died peacefully in his sleep at age seventy-seven.

Still holding the letter, Patrick closed his eyes and remembered an August afternoon with his father, sitting beside a haystack in one of their fields. They had put down the pitchforks to enjoy a cup of tea. Somehow, they had gotten to a conversation about death and dying.

Father said, "I pray when me time comes, that I just go to sleep. Your mother suffered so . . ." Pat listened thoughtfully. Then he whispered the question. The question that had been in his heart forever.

"Father, did Mam die because of me? Because of my birth?"

"No son, she did not. If there is one true thing you will ever know in this life, it is this. Your mother died from a fever, not childbirth. You need to know that she loved you very much."

Pat smiled at the warm memory. He tapped the letter against his fingers, opened his eyes and said aloud to no one, "You got your wish, Father. It was peaceful."

Paddy's death and the news that Johnny and Bridget now had seven children raised questions for Pat and he began to examine his life. He had sailed the Atlantic three times, survived the Great War, adopted a new country and had a secure future with his new position. Yet, he had no one special in his life and at the end of the day he came home to his empty room at the boarding house. He began to search deep inside to find his spirit. It was not too late to see Johnny and Bridget. He began to plan.

PART II

THE COTTAGE

Clareboy
Christmas Season 1923

MOLLIE WAS FEELING confident this morning. She was off to the town of Kilnaleck to cash her Grandmother Keogh's pension check and on the return trip, purchase some supplies at the local shop. Kilnaleck was a three-mile walk but Mollie enjoyed these monthly treks and approached each one with a sense of adventure. Today, grandmother had given her explicit instructions.

"Don't forget to remind the shopkeeper that we sent eight dozen eggs this week instead of six. That should make up the difference for the extra baking supplies. What would Christmas be without cookies and a Christmas cake?"

"Aye Granny. I can't wait for Christmas." replied Mollie in her usual competent voice. Mollie took her errand job seriously and listened attentively to all the instructions.

"Dress warm, child. Do you want a cardigan of mine? 'Tis damp this morning."

"No thanks, Granny. I'm grand. I'll be back by four o'clock. See you then."

Mollie started her three-mile walk by cutting diagonally across Grandmother's field and exiting onto the main road next to the widow Ennis' house. As Mollie approached the road, the widow called out to her.

"Mollie dear. Over here." The widow waved to the eleven-year-old, afraid Mollie had not heard her. Mollie thought it was unusual but she responded to the woman's wave.

"Hello, Mrs. Ennis."

"Mornin', Mollie. Would you do me a kind favor in the town today? Here is a six pence. Buy some sweets for yourself and your younger sisters and brothers. I wanted some little thing for the Christmas stockings and God only knows when I will see the shops again. Me arthritis is dreadful."

Mollie didn't respond. She just stared at the widow with wide eyes.

"Is something wrong?" asked the widow.

"No, no. I'll do it," coughed Mollie. She took the coin, tucked it in the pocket of her dress and turned in the direction of town.

"I wonder what that face was all about?" said the widow as she closed her cottage door against the damp mist of December.

Mollie hurried away from the cottage. She needed to find a place to sit. Could it be true? Had adults been putting the goodies in the stockings all along? Was there no Father Christmas? Crushed with the widow's news, she would have to wait until she got home to speak with Mam, without the younger children around. She continued to the post office, collected Granny's pension check and cashed it at the bank.

On the journey home, the Sweeney shop was cozy when Mollie stepped inside. There was a turf fire burning in the corner and it was a nice change from the dampness outside.

The owner, Mr. Sweeney, got out his ledger while Mollie shook out her coat and warmed her hands.

"I'm here for Granny Keogh" called Mollie over her shoulder.

"I'll just be a minute" answered the clerk. With a flip of the pages, he was soon at the Keogh account. Running his index finger down the column, he looked up and said, "You've got credit for eight cartons of eggs this week. What supplies will you be needing?"

Mollie handed him the list of supplies with the Christmas baking items added to the bottom. While Mr. Sweeney assembled the supplies on the counter, Mollie searched the display counter for the goodies she needed to purchase for the widow. She found some licorice in the shape of a clay pipe with little red dots for the glow of tobacco. There were some hard candies in different flavors and individual candy canes. She would have liked to pick something made of chocolate but with six youngsters to buy for, the six pence only stretched so far.

"Granny has a fine order today. I can tell she is truly in the Christmas spirit!" said Mr. Sweeney. "Mollie, can you carry all of this? It is still a good walk home." Mollie nodded her reply.

In the meantime, several neighbors arrived and there was a great deal of excited chatter over the upcoming Christmas holiday. Pleasantries exchanged, regards were sent to Mollie's parents and grandmother. In a few minutes, the order was packed and ready to go. The shopkeeper offered Mollie a raspberry sweet along with a cheerful "Merry Christmas." Warm from the fire and pleased with the treat from Mr. Sweeney, Mollie left the shop and continued towards home. She was anxious to speak to Mam about Father Christmas.

The days before Christmas moved slowly for the children

until it was the day before and the children were busy digging turnips from the backfield. Although the earth was cold to the touch, it was soft enough for the little fingers to move it easily.

"I've got two round ones," Bridgie called to John.

"And I have three. Just a few more and we'll have enough for the windows and the mantle," John replied. They were planning to hollow out the center of the turnips to make candle holders. Mother had already made the holiday candles and the children were excited about decorating the cottage. They planned to put a candle in each window and a series of nine across the shelf above the hearth.

When tea was purchased at the shop, it came wrapped in red tissue paper. Mam saved this tissue all year and today the children would string it, alternating with holly leaves, until they created a long chain.

The next step was to string the holly chains around the picture frames, over the doorway, and the cupboard. They had colored streamers from the shop to cross like the letter x on the top of each window. Then they would display the Christmas cards and postcards from America and Scotland on the mantel.

Grandmother Keogh and Bridget were busy with the cookies and Christmas cake made with raisins and currants soaked in rum. The activities of the season were a distraction for Grandmother who still missed her husband John. He had passed away the August before at the age of eighty. Watching her excited grandchildren was a joy and sharing the cooking with her daughter, Bridget, made the days a little easier. The two women were planning a special Christmas dinner with turkey, potatoes, turnips and onions in a white sauce. To finish the meal, there would be a treat for the children, red gelatin and rice pudding.

Margaret Mary McSherry Keogh
Clareboy, Age 92

The children could hardly wait for the darkness of night to arrive. Little Maggie spoke what all the children were thinking. "Mam, can we light the candles now? Please, please, it is almost dark outside." Grandmother and Bridget looked at each other and smiled.

"Yes, let's light the candles but be sure all your brothers and sisters are here before we begin." Well, that was all that needed to be said. The children were scrambling from outside and inside the cottage to gather around the hearth. Da took an old candle and lit it from the fire. He and mother recited the traditional prayer and passed the lit candle to Patrick, the oldest. He lit one of the candles on the mantel and passed the flame to Mollie and she passed it to John. This continued to Bridgie, Maggie, and Larry until the two youngest, Rose and James Joseph needed assistance from Da. He lifted each one up into his arms and supported their hands as they reached for a candle. Grandmother then lit the candle that had been added for her. Once all the candles were lit, the children clapped with delight and then just as quickly ran outside to see the effect of the candles in the yard. Then, it was back into the cottage to sit and admire all the decorating they had done during the day. The extra candles provided a wonderful glow to the room.

Earlier in the day, the children pulled out their stockings to hang by the fire for Father Christmas. Although the magic hour had not yet arrived, they held the stockings close, as if that would make time move faster and they could get on with tacking them in place. Eventually, the hands of the clock moved to eight, the stockings were hung with fanfare and the younger children were tucked into bed. Mam let the two oldest, Patrick and Mollie, gather the treats and stuff the stockings. Mollie spoke to Patrick.

"How many years did you know?"

"Only last year and Mam said not to tell."

"I suppose it will be fun watching the little ones."

"Wait 'til morning. You will see for yerself."

Christmas morning was a happy occasion as the delighted children found the sweets and perhaps a penny. After Mass, everyone returned to the cottage for the Christmas feast. Later that day and on into the evening, there was the traditional visiting among neighbors. At bedtime, the children collapsed into their beds, exhausted from the excitement of the day. Johnny and Bridget sat by the quiet of the hearth, sharing the tidbits of news gathered from all the visitors, content with another Christmas Day and the glow of the Christmas candles.

The Forge, Clareboy
Spring 1927

There was tension and terror in the hills around Kilnaleck. A week earlier, the springtime evening had begun as usual with a small group of people gathered outside Paul's shop at the Crossroads. Someone was playing the tin whistle when the merriment ceased. A neighbor man came into view, half-running, half-limping towards the shop, blood running down his leg. His voice was hoarse from yelling. He had difficulty getting the words out of his mouth. As he got close to the group, he collapsed onto the road.

"Help me, help me, someone please. Me wife's been shot. The baby too. Jesus, Mary and Joseph, someone help us, please, please. Oh, God."

The men gathered him up and took him inside the shop. Two others ran for the priest and the three men ran together to the farmhouse. When they arrived, it was too late to help the neighbor's wife. She lay in a pool of blood. The baby, shielded by his mother's body, had survived the attack.

The local talk was of nothing but the murder. A new rumor would start each day about why and who. Some said there were several shooters wearing masks. Others said it was one madman, a stranger just passing through the area. Others believed it was related to the independence movement and the shooting was a warning to all.

The police were determined to find the guilty. They questioned everyone, including the children. They visited the school and took some children to the station for questioning. They approached other children with questions as they walked to school. They stopped adults outside the church, the shop, and the post office. They went to every cottage.

Knowing that the forge was a gathering place and source of local gossip, the police decided to place an undercover man inside. They came to Johnny and Bridget's cottage late one night. Johnny had no choice; he had to cooperate or close the forge. The Sargent did most of the talking.

"We need you to act normal. If the men ask who the stranger is, tell them it is a blacksmith in training. The less you say about him the better. He will assist you as part of his story. This man's job is to stay disguised and listen to anything that might help us find the killer."

When Johnny went out to the forge next morning, the undercover man was already waiting for him. It made Johnny nervous and he prayed to God that the police would find the information elsewhere. He worked his usual routine but his mind was busy thinking of consequences. What if the police did hear something? Surely, the men would know it came from the forge. His neighbors would never trust him again. It would not matter that his hand was forced by the guarda. The neighbors would be angry and he and his family would pay a price.

The first morning moved along smoothly. None of the customers asked about the stranger. When it came time for dinner at noon, Johnny did not eat in the house with Bridget, as was his routine. Instead, he ate in the forge. Bad enough he felt compelled to offer the guarda food; he did not want to invite him into his home. In addition, there was the issue of the children. If a stranger came into the house, there would be more questions to answer.

Johnny let out a sigh of relief when the day was finished.

His back and neck were sore from tension. His emotions were confused and he hated the thought of getting up tomorrow and doing this again. He closed the forge and headed for the cottage.

There were no questions from the children that night and the evening passed quietly. The next day was a little easier for Johnny and by the end of the week, he was beginning to appreciate the extra pair of hands in the forge.

One windy afternoon when several farmers were waiting for Johnny at the forge, Bridget sent Mollie out to the waiting men with a handful of mugs and an old teapot. The hot drink passed around amid smiles and nods of thanks.

"What are ye doing home today, Mollie? Shouldn't you be at school, lass?"

Mollie's expression turned serious as she responded, "I've not been going to school this year. Granny Keogh is sick so I've been staying at her cottage to help. Father says I can go back to school next year. But did you hear the good news? There's talk of Uncle Pat coming home for a visit."

"That's great news. He must be a grand Yankee by now. Sure he's been away almost twenty years! I wonder what he'll think of us folk, still in the same place and only our gray hair or lack of it, to show our progress. I wonder if New York has changed him?"

Mollie started to collect the cups when she heard her baby brother Barney crying in the distance. She left what she was doing to go and check on the toddler. As she approached, Mollie could see her mother bending down to pick up the crying child. Mollie saw pain on her mother's face as Bridget's free hand grabbed at an imaginary spot on her back. Mam had not been well ever since they lost little James. It was almost three years ago but Mollie remembered it clearly.

It all started with James wanting to sleep when normally he would have been running around the yard. Mam took notice but there was no real concern until James began to burn with fever. When the fever started, Mam washed him down with cold compresses. Mrs. Ennis, a neighbor and Bridget's good friend, came over to help. She took one look at James and said that Mam should send for the doctor.

By this time, all the children were home from school and a quiet hush fell on the little cottage. Father dropped his work at the forge, swung his leg over the bicycle and headed for town. It was four hours before he was able to return with the doctor.

James had been unconscious for an hour and his fever had spiked. The doctor gave the tiny body a thorough check and turned to the anxious parents.

"We've got to keep him cool. Got to break this fever. If we don't break this fever, he'll be gone by morning."

"He'll be gone," hung in the air. Mrs. Ennis broke the silence shouting commands at everyone.

"John, get more water from the well. Mollie get tea for your parents and the doctor. Bridgie and Maggie take the younger children outside to play. Patrick, go and fetch the priest. Tell him we need him here for awhile."

Everyone did as ordered but as the sun came up the next morning, the spirit of baby James silently slipped away. Mam just wasn't the same after that.

Eighteen months later, Barney was born. He was a gift that brought renewal to the house. His smiles and baby cooing chipped away at the silence. Each day the sun shone a little brighter as the children tripped over each other to help with the new addition. Mam was happy again, but losing James and bearing her ninth child began to take a toll.

"Let me take Barney for awhile," interrupted Mollie as she effortlessly lifted the youngest into her arms. Mam reached over and smoothed the hair on her oldest daughter's brow.

"You are truly God sent, Mollie. What would I do without you?" Mollie grinned back at her mother, pleased at the wonderful compliment.

They did not suspect how soon they would both be gone.

Three Months Later

Sunday mass at Drumkilly Chapel had just progressed to the sermon when everyone was taken by surprise. Expecting the sermon to be a lengthy one, the congregation settled into their seats getting as comfortable as wooden benches would allow. The altar boys took their seats on the side of the altar. The priest moved to the pulpit.

"I have been asked by the authorities to make an announcement this morning and I must say, it gives me great comfort to do so. Several men have been arrested and charged with the local murder. As I speak to you this morning, they are awaiting trial at Mt. Joy prison."

A spontaneous cheer arose from everyone inside the chapel and a moment later a second round of cheering came from the men standing outside on the front steps.

The priest continued, "Let us bow our heads and pray together for the families of all involved, victims and killers alike."

As people left the chapel that morning they were smiling with relief, nodding heads and whispering to each other. No one remembers the rest of the Mass that day, or the man from the forge who was never seen again.

Clareboy Cottage
1927

Larry stood on the earthen floor in his bare feet and quickly scanned the cottage for his shoes. Last night he had kicked them off before he nodded off to sleep in front of the fire. He could vaguely recall his father lifting him into the sleeping loft he shared with his three brothers, Patrick, John and Barney. Today, he was anxious to get into the forge to finish the surprise. He spotted his shoes under his sisters' settle bed and smiled as he remembered the fun of the evening before.

There had been several neighbors in to the cottage to chat

with the folks. Before long, the singing had started and then the stories. Stories of the Black and Tans, the local gossip and always the stories of those who had left; the leaving was painful. It had been a grand time and Larry had fallen asleep somewhere in the middle of the shipwreck story, where even the desire to hear the ending couldn't fight the weight of his eyelids.

"Larry, want some porridge?" called his mother from her place at the side of the hearth. She had already been up for hours. The cows had been handled, chickens fed and the eggs collected. Now she was busy skimming the cream off the top of the freshly collected milk.

"Aye, Mam, that would be good. But, I've got to hurry, got some work to do in the forge."

"You know your father doesn't like you in there by yourself and he's gone to town this morning."

"But that's exactly why I have to hurry, Mam. It's a surprise, for Da, for his birthday. I can only do it when he's not here."

"I'm not sure I like the sounds of this" replied his Mother. Before Larry could respond, his sister Bridgie poked her head over the cottage half door and complained loudly that Patrick and John wouldn't let Maggie have a turn on the donkey.

Mam bent over and picked up Barney who had been toddling around between her legs.

"Come, Barney, let's go see what the others are about."

Realizing his mother was distracted, Larry wolfed down the porridge, laced up his shoes and ran into the forge. Mam saw his back as he ducked into the forge and decided to say nothing.

Larry was a sensitive kid who always seemed to care about things more than his brothers and sisters. He was easy going with a generous nature. Larry was the one to mend a broken doll for his younger sister Rose, or complete extra chores so his older brother John could go to the football match. He had sandy colored hair, blue eyes and a huge grin that made you wonder what he knew that you did not.

But childhood wasn't always easy for the ten-year-old boy

who was one of eight. He was a sickly child with a constant cough and often suffered from fevers and chills. His parents worried about his health and frequently checked on him. This habit of his parents embarrassed Larry and caused all kinds of teasing from the others. They accused him of being Mam's favorite.

Right now, what Larry wanted more than anything else in the world was to finish the forge sign he had been working on for weeks. He stoked the fire in the forge until it raged with the heat he needed to bend the strong metal bars. He hammered each stroke with care and paused often to suck some air into his lungs. He could feel the muscles in his forearms getting stronger each week, but they weren't growing fast enough for Larry. He wanted muscles like his father and his brothers, John and Patrick. He was convinced that one day he would be as strong as the rest of them.

He moved the glowing metal from the fire to the pail of cold water. The steam rose up and surrounded his entire head with fog. He loved this part the best and hesitated for a moment before removing the newly shaped metal. His thoughts wandered to the power of fire. Fire over iron. He used to think there was nothing stronger than iron.

Just then, the metal bar slipped through the tongs to the earthen floor and instinctively, he bent to pick it up.

Everyone heard the scream and came running. Patrick, the oldest, arrived first. He grabbed Larry's wrist and pushed the burned hand into the bucket of water. His Mam came next and called out for Mollie to get some clean cloth and the healing salve. For the next few moments no one spoke. Larry grit his teeth and held his breath. He did not want to cry. He would prove to them all that he was strong.

Later that day, Larry and Mam sat together by the hearth. Mam amazed Larry. How did she always know what do? She was gentle with the bandaging and gentle with the reprimand.

"What will we tell your father?" she asked Larry as he sipped a cup of tea. Mam's tea was always good but today, it was especially soothing.

"Don't know," replied Larry in a whispered voice.

"How about the truth?" asked Mam.

"It's bad enough that I've burned me hand, Mam. Please don't ask me to tell the whole story. It'll spoil the surprise." Larry's eyes were pleading. His mother thought about the situation before responding.

"I don't like to lie to anyone, not to mention your father""

"Maybe we could just tell him that I burned me hand in the hearth. Please don't tell him I burned it in the forge," begged Larry.

"Well, I am not going to make the decision for you. You think about it for awhile. Father won't be home until dark and by then you'll know the right thing to say."

Da had been like a raging bull when he heard. What was Larry doing in the forge? By himself? No one with a logical answer? And Larry not able to look him in the eye with a good explanation.

"Can't leave this farm for a day without something going wrong."

That night, Da helped change the bandage. The anger that had been so consuming disappeared when he saw the condition of his son's hand. He silently admired the boy for not whimpering and gave him a nod that said all is forgiven.

After the children were asleep, Johnny looked at his wife, and asked, "Bridget, did you not see the smoke rising from the forge and know someone was about in there?"

Bridget busied herself with a pot to avoid his look and answered carefully. "No, Johnny, I never saw the smoke this morning."

It took about a week for Larry's burn to begin to heal. On this rainy morning, Mam announced that Larry's school holiday was over. He should hurry and be ready for school with the others. There was the usual morning commotion in the small cottage. With Mollie and Patrick helping at home, there were five to get off to school, Bridgie, John, Larry, Maggie and Rose. Barney, only two, would watch with wide blue eyes as the morning ritual took place.

Father was already lighting the fire in the forge. He would grab his cup of tea each morning before the children were under foot and disappear to the early morning calm across the yard. This was his favorite time of day. He would light the fire and slowly coax it to a roar with the bellows. Then, while the fire expanded itself, he would walk, teacup in hand, to survey his fields. It wasn't a large farm by village standards but it was adequate for him and his family. His father Paddy had seen to that, like his father before him. "A man needs to have his land," his father would tell him. "It is good to be a smithy, but never lose the land." And so it had been, through the generations, that this farm and forge was Lynch land. He could feel it under his boots and crumble the earth between his fingers and know with certainty that it was his. Sometimes he thought of his brother, Pat, in New York. He wondered how different things might have been if Pat had never left. After all these years, he still missed his brother.

This morning, the rain was a gentle kind of mist. It didn't lash at you like most rain. Instead, it fell softly, silently and smelled sweet from the hay. It was the reason for the emerald hills in the distance and the rushing streams leading to Lake Sheelan.

Johnny was contemplating which field to use for hay and which for potatoes when he heard the children call to him across the distance, "Bye, Da, the eggs are collected, see you later." Johnny responded with his usual message, "Mind the teacher, children." And they were off!

The children walked to school the way most children do, half skipping and walking, running sometimes. They wore no shoes and were delighted. Winter would come soon enough and with it the restraining leather shoes that cramped your toes and slowed your freedom. Rose, the youngest going to school, was called Dodie and because of her size, always trailed a bit behind the others. As usual, it was Larry who circled back to hustle her along.

The teacher, Mrs. Nell Reilly, was just beginning to assemble her flock of students as the Lynch children arrived at the gate of the one room schoolhouse. It was the custom for the younger children to sit on the right side of the room while the older children took their positions on the left. The room was heated with a small stove that was placed midway between the front and back of the small area. During the winter, its warmth was provided through the generosity of the families who took turns contributing a block or two of turf each day. Forward and to the right of this stove was a second doorway, which led outside to a short path and eventually, the outhouse.

Once the morning assembly activities were completed, the teacher took attendance. When Larry's name was called, he reached over to Mrs. Reilly with his good hand and delivered the note from Da explaining his injury. The note also requested that Larry be allowed to stay inside during lunch to soak his hand and reapply the gauze. Mrs. Reilly nodded her head and Larry returned to his place on the bench. It was an uneventful morning and the instruction followed the expected routine. The young group would do sums and math while the older students would read with the teacher. After an hour, the groups switched activities and the teacher would move to the opposite side of the room. Sometimes, the older children would be dispersed among the younger ones and they would read in pairs. The children relished this activity and it never came often enough for them. On this day, it was not part of the plan.

Larry bit his lip through most of the morning; his hand was beginning to grow warm beneath the bandage. He tried to concentrate on his work. He wanted to last until lunch. At noon, the class was dismissed. Mrs. Reilly prepared the bucket for Larry and had some chitchat with him as his hand found relief in the cool well water. Bridgie brought Larry his lunch and John poked his head around the doorway, "How're ya doin', lad?"

But the calm of the morning was not to last. As the afternoon session got underway, Mrs. Reilly's patience began to wane. Two of the older boys were reprimanded for laughing and a third was corrected for not knowing the lesson. The scene was set for trouble when Larry made the mistake of talking when he should have been listening. Mrs. Reilly took the sally rod that was handy and lashed out at Larry. She hit him ten lashes across his outstretched hands. Larry didn't make a sound but the searing pain on his injured hand made his face contort and his throat tighten.

John watched in horror as his younger brother took the beating. John's fists clenched and his eyes narrowed with disgust from the other side of the room.

Time stood still for Larry. The room was spinning and there was a roar in his ears. Suddenly, his stomach began to lurch and everything he had eaten earlier came pouring out of his mouth in convulsive spurts.

The children sitting near him began to howl with sounds of disgust. John took advantage of all the commotion. He sprung from his seat, jumped over the benches in his way, ducked his head under Larry's armpit and in one swift movement had Larry over his shoulder. He ran for the door and in a moment, both boys were gone.

When John and Bridget heard what had happened in the Schoolhouse, they agreed that the children should not return. They kept a united front and did not send the children back to school.

The children were amazed. Their parents had always valued schooling. Now, instead of jumping with joy at the prospect of an unexpected school holiday, the children sat confused, looking at one another, sensing the seriousness of the situation. Afraid of saying the wrong thing, the children said nothing.

A week passed. Three weeks passed. By now, the children were settling into a daily routine. The chores were reassigned so everyone had something. Each night the children worked under the single paraffin lamp. There was reading to be done and numbers for those too young to read.

At the beginning of the fourth week, the local guarda arrived at the cottage. Young John was the first to spot the uniform cycling down the lane towards the cottage. He ran for Da.

"Someone's coming, could be a soldier, maybe a guarda."

"Yes, son, I've been expecting the guarda. It'll be about school or the lack of it."

Sure enough, the local guarda familiar with the location of the forge, headed straight for the double wide door. Da kept working, he didn't look up.

"Mornin' Johnny."

"Mornin' Bourke. They'll not be going back. It takes a mean son-of-a bitch to use the rod on a boy's open hands but to do it on top of the burn! You should have seen the flesh! Me and the wife are together."

" 'tis a terror, it is," agreed Bourke taking off his uniform hat and scratching the back of his head.

"Aye. 'Twill be a cold day in hell before my children cross the threshold of that schoolhouse again."

There was silence until the hammer met the anvil again. Bourke shifted his weight from foot to foot and took a deep breath before speaking again.

"Johnny lad, I need to leave this summons from the court. You'll have to tell your story to the constable. There's a date and time on the back for an appearance."

"Aye. Just leave it there."

Bourke placed the notice on the nearest shelf, called out "good luck", hopped back on the cycle and was gone as quickly as he had come.

When Johnny was sure that the guarda was safely out of earshot he spoke aloud to himself, "Sometimes a man has to do what a man has to do."

Johnny and Bridget appeared at the courthouse in Cavan Town on the appointed date. After much discussion between the parents and the judge, a compromise was reached. The children would return to school but not to Ardkill and Mrs. Reilly. They would walk a little further to Drumkilly National School where Owen O'Hannon was the teacher.

Clareboy
1928

It was a brilliant June morning when Johnny hitched the pony to the trap and prepared for his ride to Cavan Town. His brother's coach was due to arrive in Cavan Town from Dublin around noon. Bridget came out of the cottage with a basket of homemade brown bread slathered with butter.

"These are for the two of you. Sure, I know you'll be stopping for a pint before heading home but don't be delaying too long. Remember I've got a cottage of excited children here that will be waiting and watching . . . not to mention meself! I can't believe we are going to see Pat again after seventeen years. How grandfather would have enjoyed this day!"

John waved his hand in the air interrupting her lengthy goodbye, "I'll have him here by dark, 'tis a promise." He climbed onto the trap, sat sidesaddle and gave the pony a "click, click" to get moving.

The coach arrived a half hour late and as the passengers jumped down, the brothers recognized each other instantly. Before the first pint was finished, it was as if Pat had never left.

News spread that Pat was home and the cottage lane became a hive of activity with neighbors stopping by. The children sat in awe and tried to absorb Patrick's every word about his life in New York and his army war experiences. They had never met anyone as grand as Uncle Pat before and they were afraid to stand too close. His American-made clothing and the gold pocket watch dangling at the end of the shiny chain were something they had never seen on a family member before. They tried to make themselves invisible so Mam wouldn't shoo them away saying they were creating a nuisance. At the same time, they vied for Pat's attention, telling him riddles they had heard in school or wanting to show him something on the farm. Pat enjoyed the attention from the children although he did not quite know how to relate to them. He watched his brother's easy manner around the children and tried a clumsy imitation.

There had been a lot of catching up to do. The brothers fell into their old behavior patterns. They went to the football matches. Johnny played and Pat cheered from the side. Pat bought a bicycle in Cavan Town and together the men rode to Kilnaleck, Drumavaddy, Crosserlough and Ballinaugh. They laughed about the old football jersey that brought Johnny and Bridget together and reminisced about the early days with grandfather. One weekend they took the train to Dublin for a hurling match. On another, the three adults took the children to a carnival in Cavan Town. They all went to the chapel together on Sundays and afterwards visited the graveyard. Pat arranged for a Mass to be said for his parents, Rose and Paddy. Evenings were spent next to the fire with poteen added on Saturdays.

Late one afternoon as Pat helped Johnny close up the forge, he began to think aloud. "Johnny, do you remember the midwife, Teresa O'Malley?"

"Aye, I do."

"Is she still in Cavan Town?"

"She is."

"What is she about these days?"

"Getting old like the rest of us. Still getting around. Works in a shop at the far end of the town. Haven't talked to her since she came to Kilnaleck for the market last year."

"I've been thinking that now I'm on me feet, I would give her a little something for all her help when I was young. What do you think?"

"'Tis a splendid idea. Very generous. She is a strange one though. She walks around like she owns the town instead of being a shop clerk coming from nothing any better than the rest of us."

"Sure, she was always that way."

"You know, don't you, that Father paid her at the time. I'm sure a gift would be nice but mind you, some folk think you are a millionaire because you can make a trip from New York. Mind your wallet, Patrick, don't be taken advantage of. Sure you were far too generous with the priest last week. Two shillings is plenty for a mass. His teeth almost fell out when you gave him the pound note. Do you think he is always falling over himself to welcome us in the chapel? Sure there's been a serious attitude adjustment since you arrived. I don't be wanting to tell you what to do brother, but it will pain me to see you taken advantage of."

"You're right, Johnny lad. I should have asked you before we went to the chapel. They say a fool and his gold are soon parted. I'm pleased for the advice."

"Aye, but you're no fool, just a generous man with a thoughtful way."

The night of Pat's welcome home coeli, neighbors began to drift in around nine in small groups. The fiddler, Andy McGuire, arrived at ten and by midnight the cottage was overflowing with the crowd getting thick in the outside yard. Vast quantities of porter flowed easily from the barrel tap. Everyone was singing and dancing. This party would be one to remember!

In spite of all the noise, Barney had fallen asleep on his mother's lap. She put him down for the night on her bed and returned to the party. The crowd danced the hornpipe and one group organized a set. Bridget's mother, Mary Keogh, now eighty-six years, sang an Irish ballad of the Black and Tans. The applause and shouts could be heard three counties away. The younger children, Larry, Rose and Maggie ran in and out amongst the crowd trying to imitate the dancers. Patrick, Mollie, John and Bridgie were busy with friends from school.

As the party progressed into the wee hours of the morning, Seamus Reilly began to look for his father to go home.

"Ah, he can't take the por tah anymore" said an elderly neighbor with no teeth, waving his hand in a sign of disgust. "He passed out on the bed hours ago."

Seamus and Bridget went in search of the old man. To Bridget's horror, several men had passed out on the bed amidst a pile of coats, jumpers and vests that had been shed by the overheated revelers. Bridget began to scream.

"Get up, get off, the baby's under there!" She pushed, shoved and pulled. But the weight of the unconscious men was too much for her. No one moved. Bridget began to panic. She screamed for her husband, "Johnny, Johnny come quick! The baby is smothered under here!"

Johnny came running with Pat and with several others managed to roll the drunks onto the floor and throw the coats into the air. Johnny got to the baby first and rolled him onto his back. He put his ear to the baby's chest. Baby Barney startled by the sudden movements and the yelling started to wail at the top of his lungs.

"Thanks be to God," whispered Bridget as she clutched the baby close to her breast. Johnny put his arms around them both and broke into a hearty laugh. At first the others just stared at him but one by one they felt relief and joined in the laughter at the scene. The drunks were still sleeping, the clothing was everywhere and the baby was fine. The fiddler had never heard Bridget's screams so the dancing hadn't missed a beat.

Someone jumped out of the crowd and pulled Pat into the middle of a large circle that was forming. Arm in arm, the men, women and children began to sway together in one unbroken circle as they surrounded Pat and sang,

Welcome home, welcome
Come on in and close the door
You've been gone too long,
Welcome, you're home once more.

For a moment Pat's eyes began to get moist and he wondered why he had ever left this magical place. What lights the spark in a man's soul and makes him leave the place he loves, where he is loved? He thought back to the night he sailed from Galway Bay when he whispered to himself, "look to the future, don't look back." How foolish young men can be. He was looking back now and loving it all.

The next morning saw not a stitch of work from anyone in the cottage. It was noon before anyone began to awake, including little Barney. Amidst porridge, bread and tea, everyone chatted about the successful coeli.

"I can't thank all of you enough," Pat elaborated with outstretched arms. "It was a colossal night. Sure the good times are not nearly enough in this life, but I will remember this night always."

Looking around the little group he picked up Barney and lifted him high into the air, "And you little fella scared the B'Jaysus out of us!" With that said, everyone laughed and enjoyed the warmth that comes from being together.

Patrick and Mollie, the two oldest children, were going to be in charge of the cottage for the afternoon. Bridget and Johnny and Pat were off to a feis in Cavan Town. There was a fiddler and a piper coming from County Donegal. The musicians had grown up nearby and moved away the same year that Pat had left for Galway. The adults were excited about a day out as well as a reunion with former schoolmates.

Bridget began to prepare a flask of tea and some sandwiches for the outing as well as a dinner for the eight children staying behind. Pat interrupted her, "Bridget, let me treat you to dinner today. You are always working and taking care of us. Today is a day out!" Turning to Mollie and Patrick he said, "These two fine youngsters can handle the young lot, and I'm sure they won't starve."

"We'll be fine," replied Mollie.

At that point, Johnny came into the kitchen. The pony and trap were ready. He put his hands firmly on his wife's shoulders, turned her around and began to gently push her out the door. As Bridget walked forward she turned her head to the side and called last minute directions to Mollie and Patrick.

"Keep a sharp eye on Barney and Rose. Patrick don't forget to bring water from the well before it gets dark and Mollie use the spuds in the black kettle first and there's chicken in the cupboard."

"Aye. We know. We know. Just go on now," replied Mollie.

"Have a good day," called Bridgie with Barney in her arms. "Wave bye to Mam," she told the little boy.

"Enjoy the music," called Larry. The pony started up the lane surrounded by a pack of children, cheering and calling out goodbye.

The feis was extremely crowded. The fine weather had encouraged everyone to leave the chores behind and come out for the day. There were food stalls set up along the side streets and a huge stage had been erected in the center of the square. There were step dancers in traditional costumes and musicians of every kind. The music groups each took a turn performing to the enthusiastic crowd. People responded to the rhythms by clapping in time or dancing in the roadways. Bridget was enjoying everything as her eyes moved quickly to absorb the entire scene. She had forgotten how much fun a feis could be. She danced with Johnny until her heartbeat demanded a rest. "The music is fine indeed," she puffed to Johnny. "And did you hear those voices?"

"The voices of angels, surely," replied Johnny as he took out his handkerchief and wiped the perspiration off his upper lip. "Let's find Pat and get something to eat."

The crowd was expanding as people continued to arrive. They pushed through the ring of dancers and headed for the clearing ahead where they could get a better view and find Pat. As they approached, they spotted Pat standing with his back to them and a short woman facing him. The woman was pointing her finger at Pat and yelling in a loud voice. Johnny recognized her as Teresa O'Malley, the midwife. As Bridget and Johnny got closer, they were able to decipher the woman's angry words.

"Look at you now. You would be nothing without me. I reared you. I saved your life! What have you given me? Let every person have his just reward, the Bible says. Where is mine? You are a stingy son of a bitch!"

Bridget and Johnny stood still. Bridget's mouth fell open. When Teresa spotted them, she turned to leave, but called out one more threat. "This is not the last of it. You'll be hearing from me again, you worthless, ungrateful piece of rubbish." She strode off in a huff and disappeared into the crowded street below.

The trio stood dumbfounded. No one spoke for several minutes. Pat broke the silence. "She wanted money from me. No, she was demanding it. She got me so angry I told her to go to hell."

"But you had planned to give her some money," answered Johnny.

"Aye, I planned a gift, not an obligation. Who is she to tell me what I should give her? She made me crazy with her demanding. Once she got me anger up, it was all over. I told her to go to hell. She never asked me how I was getting on, just came over like a charging bull. Sure, we both know that father took care of things with her. But even as a kid, she saw me as pound notes, nothing more. I couldn't wait for the day I would leave her place. She was always nasty and now age has made her bitter. Poor soul, she'll never be content."

They stood in silence another few minutes trying to make sense of the scene. Patrick tried to change the mood. In his most cheerful voice he said, "Forget her. Let's not ruin this great day. Let's have dinner!" He moved between Bridget and Johnny and put an arm around the shoulder of each. They had only walked a short distance when they heard shouting behind them. They turned and there were the friends from Donegal. There was great excitement and lots of hugs going round. The group went to dinner together.

Aside from the encounter with Teresa O'Malley, the day had been delightful. They rode home slowly enjoying the twilight of a long summer evening. It would not be dark until eleven. Without realizing it, the conversation took on the quiet mood of the evening and they spoke in hushed tones. The crickets chirped and the gentle breeze carried the sweet smell of summer flowers. Their bodies swayed gently with the motion of the cart as the horse made his way back home without direction from the driver.

They rode silently now, each with private thoughts. Pat was thinking how bright the stars shone in the sky, so different from New York. Bridget began to realize how much she had needed a day away from her happy brood of children. She was feeling refreshed. Johnny thought about the day when sadness crept into his heart. It was almost time for Pat to leave again. The leaving would be painful.

Teresa O'Malley was determined to make good on her threat. She visited several solicitors in Cavan Town but with no success. They each told her that thirty-three years had passed since she gave her services and whether she was telling the truth or not about money owed, the time for a legal solution had expired. Eventually, she found a young solicitor with little experience and convinced him to plead her case against Patrick Lynch. The solicitor prepared the papers and posted them to Patrick Lynch, Clareboy.

The summer would soon turn to fall. It was time for farmers and villagers alike to prepare for the upcoming winter. Everyone was off to the bog to cut the bricks of turf, stack them to dry in the sun and eventually cart the supply home. Turf would be needed for the fire to spread warmth and to cook meals throughout the long winter months. The backbreaking work was softened by the social gatherings at the bog. Neighbors formed groups and worked side by side. Tea breaks were enjoyable and sometimes there would be a harmonica or tin whistle. These were happy days spent in the sunshine. The children helped with the stacking until they were old enough to master the skill of cutting with a slaine.

Johnny and Pat were returning with the cart and half a dozen children when Bridget came out to meet them in the lane.

"How was your day?" she called in an interested voice to Johnny.

"Grand altogether. Tomorrow you should come. Mary Teresa is planning to come with Tom and she wants to see you."

"Sure would be a wonderful chance to visit. I'll ask if Nora can keep Barney and Rose."

Bridget had been expecting the children to come home with half of the bog on their faces and clothing. She had a huge caldron of rainwater warming on the fire all afternoon. She set out the large tin bathing tub in front of the hearth and added the warm water and a bar of homemade soap. One by one the children took turns in the bath, scrubbed and returned to their normal color.

A neighbor named Patrick Lynch came down the lane on horseback. "Evenin', Johnny," he called from his perch atop the saddle.

"This notice came today, but I believe it to be for your brother. It is addressed to Patrick Lynch, but it's not for me." He handed the envelope over and continued.

"How was the bog? I had to work on me shed. Hope to get there tomorrow. Aren't we lucky with this spell of dry weather? Can't remember an August like this."

"Aye, you're so right! Thanks for bringing down the letter."

"Sure it was on me way. I'm off to the shop."

Johnny went into the barn where Pat was unloading the cart and stacking the turf against the west wall. "Here's a letter for you. It was delivered to the wrong house." He handed it over. "Can't imagine what that could be," puzzled Pat.

He began to read the letter while Johnny took over stacking the turf. "Oh, bloody hell!" cried Pat. "That crazy woman is at it again. It's a legal paper to force payment for my care. I will not be forced into this. Tomorrow I'll go to town and get this action dismissed. She gets me so angry!"

Johnny stopped what he was doing. "Teresa again?"

"Aye. A right pain in the arsh she turned out to be!"

When Bridget heard of the situation, she was embarrassed. "Of all the pieces of mail to go astray, it had to be that! Now anyone who didn't hear of her yelling fit in the town will know about the legal papers. I don't like the neighbors knowing our business. I can't believe she found a solicitor to help her. Such rubbish!"

"I'm sorry I've brought you shame," replied Pat.

"It is not you, Pat. 'Tis the crazy old woman. It will get worked out. No judge will listen to her ramblings." But the relaxed mood of the early evening was lost.

Pat set out for town early the next morning. He decided to visit the solicitor first. When the young man heard Pat's version of the story, he agreed to withdraw the claim. Pat's second stop was the cottage of Teresa O'Malley.

The last week of Pat's visit was a blur. The same hum that invaded the lane when he arrived had returned. There were people coming and going all hours of the day and night.

The morning of his departure for New York, Patrick hugged and kissed each one of the eight children and lingered for a few last words with Bridget. He had always been fond of her and he appreciated her warm welcome that made his visit so enjoyable. So, with kisses and a wave, and Johnny driving the horse and cart, the brothers ambled up the lane for the last time.

New York City
September 1928

When Pat's ship pulled into the Manhattan pier, the city and the entire country were bustling. Prosperity appeared to be everywhere.

Pat settled back into his daily activity with one routine added. Every Thursday night he would write to Johnny, Bridget and the family. The strong ties of childhood were reestablished and he wanted to keep them that way.

Walking home from the trolley one winter evening, he had the thought that perhaps one of Johnny's children could come to New York. It would be wonderful to have one here with him and it could lend some financial support to Johnny. His brother had never complained of his situation but Pat was aware of the unspoken needs.

The following Thursday, when he wrote his letter to Clareboy, he included his offer to pay the boat passage for one of the children to join him in New York. He hoped his offer would be welcomed as a gift and not seen as a boastful suggestion. But Pat should have had no fears because once Johnny and Bridget received his generous offer, there was never a question about accepting it. The question was, "Who should go?"

Clareboy
October 1928

Johnny and Bridget waited for the eight sets of ears to fall asleep before they began the discussion that lasted late into the night. They talked about Patrick and Mollie. Patrick was

the oldest, Mollie the more adventurous. A boy could find work
easier; a girl needed a safer place to live. A son was needed in
the forge; Patrick didn't like the forge. Mollie, as the oldest
girl, was needed in their own household.

The thought of sending either one to New York was painful,
yet a golden opportunity not to be dismissed. Weary from the
discussion, they decided to tell Patrick and Mollie together. As
Johnny blew out the lamp and settled into bed, Bridget turned
and asked him, "Johnny, do you suppose neither one will want
to go?"

The following week Mollie had the strange sensation that
her parents were staring at her. She was helping with the baby
when she felt her mother's gaze and it made her stop and look
up. Bridget returned Mollie's startled expression with a smile.

When Mollie went into the forge to call father for supper,
she thought that he looked at her differently, as if he was
deciding if he liked her dress or not. Mollie shrugged her
shoulders and asked, "Is something wrong, Da?"

"No child. Just can't believe how my oldest daughter has
gown to be such a fine young lady."

On Friday morning, when the younger children had left
for school, father stopped his work in the forge and went into
the cottage for tea. Bridget called Patrick and Mollie to join
them. Once the four were sitting around the table, father
pulled Uncle Pat's letter from his pocket.

"Uncle Pat wrote again this week. He has an interesting
offer in his letter. He is willing to sponsor one of you to join
him in New York." There was silence.

Mother continued, "It took us by surprise. We never
discussed it when he was here."

"I don't ever want to leave Ireland," said Patrick.

"I would love to go to New York," said Mollie.

Bridget and Johnny were shocked by the immediate
response of the children. How simply the decision was made.

PART III

MOLLIE

Dublin
February 1929

MOLLIE'S MOUTH ACHED and her handkerchief was squeezed into a little ball in the palm of her hand. She tried to breathe deeply and relax in the back seat of the horse and buggy, but her mind raced. She tried unsuccessfully to smooth her new dress and regain her composure.

Never had she met a man like the dentist who had just butchered her mouth. His manner was harsh and he made it quite clear to the fifteen year old that money, not his patient, was his concern.

She had been his seventh victim that morning. This greedy laggard had given up professional concern years ago. His new goal was wealth, and the hundreds of young people seeking emigration were his own means to that end. His wealth was already beginning to show in the fat folds that overhung his trousers. He laughed at his patients, their country ways, and their timid faith in his friend, O'Rourke. Yes, he must remember to send his monthly payment to O'Rourke for the business he'd sent to him. It was the least he could do for the civil servant. He considered O'Rourke a complete fool having five mouths to feed when the entire country was in a slump and hundreds leaving everyday for England and the Americas.

Mollie's horse and buggy meandered through the streets of Dublin in no great hurry. It was a nice day for the month of February and the entire city seemed to be enjoying the welcome relief from winter.

The horse came to a slow stop and the driver asked for the fare. Mollie paid the driver and held tightly to what remained. Some quick calculating told her that she had one pound left plus the return half of her train ticket.

For the second time that morning she climbed the steps to the Irish Council Offices on O'Connell Street. When she had been there earlier, Mr. O'Rourke, the medical clerk, had said she needed two teeth removed. At the time, Mary was grateful for his assistance. After all, O'Rourke was the one who had secured her the horse and buggy and told the driver where to find the dentist. However, Mollie was angry now and she intended to tell this man about her horrible experience. When she entered the building, another clerk was in O'Rourke's place.

Like most of the people her age, Mollie heard all the horror stories of what happened to new arrivals in the ports of New York and Boston. Failing your medical exam meant a return trip to home. The Irish government was attempting to limit the anguish by examining all those wishing to leave. Mollie knew this and accepted O'Rourke's statement about the dentist with confidence.

"Next!" bellowed the clerk as Mollie jumped to attention and handed him the completed form. The clerk read her papers with no trace of expression. He stamped the forms and scribbled his initials.

"Everything seems to be in order," he said as he smiled and handed her back the authorized form.

"Just one more window, lass and you'll be on your way to America." Mollie's eyes followed his pointing finger to the other side of the large hall. She thanked him and strode across the hall with a new confidence. After all, she was going to America. She'd better start looking the part. She straightened her shoulders, lifted her head with the short, brown hair framing the smooth complexion and temporarily forgot the pain in her mouth.

There were two young men ahead of Mollie but the line moved quickly. The female clerk smiled at the young woman standing before her.

"Such a young thing," the clerk thought. "This is the fourth one this morning. Will it never stop Sweet Jesus? What is to become of us, with our young leaving every day and the old folk grieving after them? The leaving is so painful."

When the clerk just seemed to stare into space, Mollie coughed to bring attention back to the matter at hand.

"Oh, excuse me," the woman said as she realized there was a lapse of time.

"All I'll be needing is your two pounds for the visa stamp."

Mollie opened her purse and started to count her coins when suddenly her mind flashed back to paying the buggy driver and she knew immediately, she did not have two pounds. Her heart jumped inside her chest and her mouth went dry. She was so close to America! How could two pounds stop her now? She fought the moisture growing behind her blue eyes and reached deep within her for the strength to reply, "I don't have two pounds." The silence was deafening and it seemed like forever before the clerk responded.

The woman's voice was gentle, "Weren't you told that you would need money today?"

The kindness in the woman's voice opened the floodgates for Mollie and she blurted out her complete story hardly stopping for air. The clerk suggested that she would hold the papers and Mollie should mail her the required fee. Mollie reached through the grillwork, squeezed the woman's hand, and carefully copied the name and address for the mailing.

Once outside the building, Mollie rested on a nearby bench. What a morning this had been. If going to America was to continue in this fashion, she would have gray hair before she reached the streets of New York.

When Mollie had not returned from Dublin by the normal bedtime, Father asked his sons, Patrick and John, to wait at the end of the lane and meet her. John gave Patrick a wink and a grin and called over his shoulder, "It's done."

The two boys left the cottage, and once they were sure no little ones were going to attempt to tag along, they headed for the back of the barn. Tucked away behind a loose board was their secret supply of fags. Patrick pulled them out and quickly tucked them in his pants pocket. The boys then walked the half mile to the end of the lane and turned right.

Convinced that they were far enough from the cottage, Patrick shared the fags and the match with John. He inhaled deeply, coughing a little. The brothers continued the next quarter mile to the road. They made themselves comfortable leaning against a small stone wall. The February night was cold but clear. The brothers didn't seem to notice. Thinking aloud, John said, "Mollie must have missed the early coach. She would be here by now. The last one puts into Cavan by nine, then she needs a cart for home. Should be any minute now."

Patrick didn't answer. He continued a steady rhythm of sucking in the smoke, tilting back his head and exhaling with a long breath. John watched him closely. John was only thirteen but he decided he was old enough to know more about what was going on in the family these days. He might be child number four but he was the second son with only Mollie and Bridgie between him and his brother. No one said there was a problem but John could sense it. He was good at that sort of thing. His sister Bridgie said he had a gift.

Tonight Patrick was unusually quiet. John spoke, "Isn't it exciting, Mollie going to New York?"

"Aye."

"Can you imagine living in a city like that?"

No answer.

"Of course, she'll have Uncle Pat to show her around."

No answer.

John kept on; "It could be scary. Not that I would be afraid, mind you. But going to a new place and not knowing anyone and trying to find a job is scary. I wonder what position Mollie could find? Uncle Pat must have something in mind."

No answer.

John summoned his courage and asked the question that was bothering him all week. He took a deep breath first. "Patrick, how come you're not going to New York? You're seventeen and you're the oldest."

"Shut your damn mouth, John."

They sat in silence for a few minutes before the horse and cart could be heard approaching from the distance. Mollie hung over the side of the cart and looked in the direction of the lane. It was a dark night but the two fags glowing in the distance were clearly visible. She was never so glad to see her brothers!

John ran over and helped Mollie off the cart. They said goodnight to the driver and the trio started down the lane. John immediately began with his list of questions. Patrick stopped him.

"Let her tell us and don't be interrupting all the time."

The next morning, Da questioned Mollie. "You didn't get it?"

Molly began her story. "I didn't have enough money . . ."

Father angrily interrupted her, "How could you not have enough money? I gave you the train ticket and three pounds, girl. The papers are two pounds, with one pound extra!" Da's face was getting red and Mollie saw the vein in his neck start to twitch. She knew what that meant; she had seen it before.

There was the time Bridgie ate a raw turnip in the south field, the way they did a hundred times, but this time, she broke her front tooth.

Mollie decided her best course of action was not to explain about O'Rourke, the horse and buggy ride and the dentist. Instead, she cut to the ending.

"The clerk said I could mail in the missing amount and she would send us the papers."

"Are you daft, girl? Who will send you the papers? They will keep the money and say it never arrived. You are too trusting! How will you ever survive in America? I thought ye knew better."

Mollie felt the tears of embarrassment well up but she stood her ground. "This is the paper I have. We send the money to this clerk. She will affix the stamp and post it back. It will save us another trip to Dublin. The clerk said it happens sometimes and there is no need to come back. Everything is in order except the fee."

Father would have none of it. He ranted and raved around the kitchen. He stomped out to the forge. He made a quick, about-face turn and came back to the house.

"Give me the damn papers, I will talk to Mr. Cullen, the agent. He will know. You don't have a brain in that head of yours."

Mollie stayed strong. She handed him the papers without flinching. Father stomped out the door again, grabbed his bicycle and began pedaling to the Cullen Agency in Cavan Town.

In the quiet space that remained after his angry exit, Mollie told her entire tale to Mam. Patrick and John, who had heard everything the night before, quietly entered the cottage and sat to listen. The younger ones, oblivious to the importance of the event, continued whatever they were doing.

As always, Mam was a good listener. She examined Mollie's mouth during the dentist part of the story and quietly listened until the conclusion.

"You handled yourself well, Mollie. You had no choice with the dentist. Your Da and I should have seen to your teeth months ago. I'm sorry. Now it is done. I haven't heard about using the post before so I am going to pray that you were given the correct information. Father wants everything to go well for you and he doesn't want Pat in America to think we can't handle a little paperwork. That's what is really burning him. Sure, everyday they are changing the regulations. Let's put wet tea leaves on that swollen gum of yours."

Mollie's sister, Bridgie, was fourteen and bursting with questions. Thrilled to have an audience for the story, Mollie sat with the tea leaves and Bridgie. Father returned just after noon.

"Mr. Cullen said there was no harm in sending through the post if Mollie had seen a plaque with the clerk's name on it that matched the name to be sent the money. What did you see, girl? Was the clerk's name posted?"

"Aye," responded Mollie.

"Then we'll send the money," decided Da.

The next two weeks were torture for Mollie. Each day she would be watching for the postman. Nothing arrived. Da had given the return mail his own deadline of fifteen days. If they did not have the papers by then, he was going to Dublin himself. On the morning of the sixteenth day, the papers arrived in the post.

"Praise God" was the only thing Da had to say. Mother wrapped Mollie in a bear hug and began to rock her oldest daughter back and forth saying, "I can't believe you are really going." The leaving will be painful.

The reality of leaving started to settle in for Mollie. At fifteen, there was a combination of excitement, fear and loneliness. She told herself how lucky she was to be going to New York. Nevertheless, some nights her mind raced with questions that had no answers. At other times, she would quietly look around trying to memorize every inch of this home and her family. God only knows when she would ever, if she would ever, return.

One elderly neighbor, a cousin of Grandmother Rose, told Mollie she was going to a place where she would never again see a blade of green grass! She did not believe him, but what should she expect? She tried to recall details of every story Uncle Pat had told her. Perhaps if she could remember the stories, they held all the answers she was seeking.

Bridget was busy sewing several new dresses for Mollie to pack in her case. As she stitched, she reminisced about her days as a seamstress and her journey to Scotland. Looking back, she was pleased to have had the experience before meeting Johnny and raising her little brood. But, America was so much further away. I wonder will I ever see Mollie again? She shook her head to dismiss such sad thoughts and focused on what needed to be done.

There was so much to do! So much to tell her eldest daughter about life before she left. Suddenly, Bridget was running out of time.

Larry was the first of four children to come running into the cottage. He was out of breath from the run to be first with the news.

"There is a pony and trap coming down the lane. A woman and a girl in it. I don't know them. We were in the field behind the Ennis cottage and took the shortcut home to tell you. The pony and trap won't be here for another while." His message delivered, he turned and ran outside to join the others.

Mother broke into laughter at the funny antics of Larry. "Time to put the kettle on for tea, we'll be having visitors. Mollie, please help me put this sewing away and clear the table." Ten minutes later, the pony and trap stopped outside the half door of the cottage.

"Are ye at home, Bridget? It's me, Maggie Gallager with my daughter, Maureen." Bridget stepped out of the cottage and smiled at the mother and daughter sitting in the trap.

"Welcome, welcome, and where else would I be in the middle of the week. Come in and have tea. What brings you out to our little corner of the world today? Surely, you don't need a blacksmith."

"I have wonderful news. Maureen is going to America with Mollie. Johnny's brother, Pat, is sending two tickets instead of one. The girls will be traveling on the same ship so I wanted to come over, chat about it, and give the girls a chance to meet each other. Sure, they'll be leaving in no time at all."

Mollie and her mother stopped short. They stood with their mouths open, gaping at the pair of women. The visitors continued through the doorway and without hesitation, took seats at the table in front of the hearth. The shocking news left Bridget and Mollie speechless. Bridget recovered first. She asked, "When did you hear all this good news?"

Maggie Gallagher continued as if she were merely talking about the weather. "Well, it seems that my sister, Teresa O'Malley, had a little chat with Pat when he was home visiting from New York last year. Pat said he would send something to Teresa and being a man of his word, he sent this ticket to Teresa for Maureen. We can't believe our good fortune." Maureen and Mollie listened as the two mothers continued the conversation.

"Maureen needs to go to Dublin immediately and get her papers. Then she needs to visit our family in Donegal, say her good-byes and pack her case. What about you, Mollie? Are you ready to go?"

"Yes. Just a few last minute things to organize."

Bridget served the tea with some biscuits from a special tin, kept for such occasions. The two girls, soon to be travelers, chatted about different teens they knew, attempting to find a common friend. Unsuccessful, they both sat quietly. Mollie had a million things to ask Maureen but she thought it best to hold her tongue in front of both mothers. When the conversation suddenly got quiet, Mollie changed the topic.

"Should I go to the forge and get Father? He will surely want to meet Mrs. Gallagher and Maureen."

"Yes, of course, and I am sure he could use a cup of hot tea," replied Mother. Mollie ran to the forge. She wanted to tell father about Uncle Pat's plan in private. She suspected that he would be as shocked as they were and would not enjoy being embarrassed in front of all the women. Father liked to assume nothing could slip past him. As Mollie spoke, Father stopped his work and shook his head in disbelief.

"I'll just wash up a little. Tell your mother I will be right there."

May 1929

They had a farewell party for Mollie the evening before she left. Her older brother Patrick could not imagine preparing to travel to New York on his own. Any feelings of jealousy that had cropped up during the last few months were gone, replaced with respect for Mollie's courage.

The morning of Mollie's departure he came to apologize.

"Sorry I was so cranky lately. I didn't know what to say to you. I'll be lost without you around here."

"Not to worry. I will miss you also."

Her brother, John and sister, Bridgie, imagined the journey was an adventure. The four youngest, Maggie, Larry, Rose and Barney talked about Mollie going to see Uncle Pat in New York, as if it were down the road.

The day of departure was a Saturday. Father hired a car and driver to take Mam, Mollie with her suitcase, Patrick and himself to Cavan Town. They were to meet Maureen at eight in the morning and from there the girls would travel together to Londonderry.

They arrived early to Cavan Town and waited about twenty minutes for the coach to arrive. Da was nervous and shifted his weight from foot to foot. "Mollie, have you forgotten anything?"

"No, I checked my case several times."

Father held Mollie. "Be careful with your ticket and your money."

Patrick hugged his sister. "Good luck and tell Uncle Pat I was asking for him."

Mam held Mollie close and whispered, "Don't forget to write to me child. I love you and I will miss you. I will pray for your safe journey. Now bless yourself."

Mollie could not respond with words but her face told it all. She had agonized over this moment for months and now it was here. She was sad and nervous but trying to be strong. She gripped the handle of her small case and climbed onboard the coach with Maureen. She waved from the window until her parents and brother were mere specks in the distance.

Maureen, still weepy, spoke first. "Do you know what time we will get to Derry?"

"I think around three," answered Mollie.

Londonderry, on the northern coast of Northern Ireland, was a ship building center with commercial and passenger traffic. It was a jewel in the British crown and it was the furthest Mollie had ever been from home.

When the girls arrived in Derry, their ship, the TSS CALIFORNIA, sat anchored in the outer harbor. The girls boarded a tender with thirty other passengers for the short trip across the bay to the steamship.

Once onboard, they were assigned to the same cabin. They located it with little difficulty and each girl dropped her suitcase of meager belongings onto the floor. They were surprised to see four bunks in the room. Exhausted, they stretched out onto the two lower bunks. A moment later, bells rang and the ship stewards called out from the corridors.

"Lifeboat drill. Everyone to the muster station. Bring your life vest and no talking." This repeated until all the cabins were empty.

The girls scrambled up four decks, found their assigned station and struggled with the bulky life vests. Ever since the Titanic tragedy in 1912, it was standard procedure to issue life vests and demonstrate to passengers where to assemble in case of emergency. All the passengers were now standing in silent rows on the port and starboard decks.

As they waited for further directions, Mollie began to absorb the details of the people collected about her. There were a few family groups and some older couples. She counted four women with infants in their arms. Mostly, it was young people in their early twenties, mostly male, mostly singles travelling alone. She looked at their clothing, the styles of their shoes, the confidence in some faces and the lack of it in others. Satisfied, she turned her attention back to the safety instructions.

As the ship continued its readiness for the voyage, Mollie felt the vibration of the powerful engines starting below deck. She heard the rattling of the metal chains as the anchor pulled upward from the seabed. Suddenly, there was a loud blast from the ship's horn and the CALIFORNIA was underway, bound for its westerly route across the Atlantic.

It was twilight and the lights of Derry were slowly disappearing from view. The only sound was of water washing against the sides of the ship. The girls stood at the rail looking out to the ocean. The lonesome sound of the horn brought all the emotions of the moment to the surface for Mollie and Maureen. They wanted to be excited but they stood quietly, each with her own thoughts and tears.

Dinner on board was at eight. Mollie and Maureen did not want to be late on the first evening. As they entered the dining area on the second deck, they silently admired the fine table settings and the comfortable chairs. Small luxuries appreciated by the blacksmith's daughter. They took their assigned seats and responded politely as one young man started the introductions at the table. A waiter soon appeared with steaming bowls. The soup and the aroma stirred their appetites after the long day of travel.

Mollie looked down at her bowl of soup just as the hot liquid began to slosh from side to side. Up one side of the bowl and down the other, the soup mimicked the motion of the sea. Mollie's stomach moved with the rhythm of the soup and the sea, up one side and down the other. She clamped her handkerchief over her mouth and made a hasty exit to the outside deck. Once at the rail, she emptied into the sea what little was in her stomach.

The seasickness continued for eight days and eight nights. Mollie moved between her bed and the ship's rail. It was impossible to walk by the dining deck without getting ill. The odors of cooking food, drifting up from the ship's galley, caused a major revival of the illness in her belly. Her throat and the muscles in her side were sore from retching. She lost weight and felt weak.

On the morning of the ninth day, the seasickness left as suddenly as it had appeared. Slowly, Mollie began to eat and enjoy the dining room. The food was nourishing and by the tenth day, she was beginning to feel normal again. She visited a gift shop on board and bought an orange. She also purchased a pink handkerchief imprinted with a picture of the TSS CALIFORNIA. She planned to mail it home to her mother when she arrived in New York.

PART IV

MICHAEL

I N THE SOUTHWEST corner of Ireland lies the County of Kerry, often referred to as The Kingdom of Kerry. Several peninsulas jut into the sea with the northernmost one, thirty miles long, named after the town of Dingle. There is only one road connecting The Dingle Peninsula to the mainland and the city of Tralee. The traveler must follow this road to the village of Camp, where the road divides with Dingle to the left and Castlegregory, Cloghane and Brandon to the right.

Very few travel the right fork. Here the road winds along the coastline, past the base of Brandon Mountain, ending abruptly above the steep cliffs of Brandon Point and the crashing waves of the Atlantic below.

To follow this story, take the right fork to Cloghane.

The Village of Cloghane
Circa 1837

Samuel Lewis, a visitor to the village in 1837, recorded that there were "thirty-five dwellings, all thatched." He also recorded that there "was a parochial church, a Roman Catholic chapel and a school." However, what Lewis did not write is perhaps more important because, in the same year, he visited Killarney and tells us there "are 7,000 inhabitants with brewing, milling and the manufacture of linen." He continues with Dunquin "gradually improving its agriculture and Ballylongford with 300 inhabitants exports corn and turf." By comparison, the description of Cloghane, with its lack of people, industry and growth, reflects the difficult situation at that time.

Cloghane Inlet, Co. Kerry

The temperature never gets too cold or too hot on this north side. The summers are cooled with the ocean breeze and the winters warmed with the currents. Snow is rare. The colors of the area are vibrant. Emerald green mountains and miles of white strand disappear into rushing blue surf. The strand wraps around the inlet resembling a half circle and nestled into the center is a cluster of houses.

It is a magnificent setting taken for granted by the locals because life in this beautiful place can be hard. It is the locals who have struggled with the rocky soil to grow meager crops. It is they who have fought for their lives with the ocean tides. It is they who have battled the wind to capture a net of fish. Life can be hard in this beautiful place.

June 1854

Michael Fitzgerald and three other lads were the first to spot the unusual movements in the water. Any other day it would have gone unnoticed but today the lads had been racing barefoot on the strand. The sand felt cool and refreshing under their feet. School would soon be out and they had the energy only thirteen-year-olds can possess. Panting loudly, they flopped down onto the sand to rest, when they noticed the large dark shadows and ripples on the surface of the usually quiet inlet. When they investigated, they discovered a large group of porpoises trapped in the shallow pool created by the outgoing tide. As the minutes passed and the tide receded, the huge creatures became more helpless.

"Run for the villagers!" Michael yelled to his companions as he sprinted quickly in the opposite direction for the fishermen. He knew they would be working near the curraghs mending the nets or repairing the boats.

"Lots of porpoises caught in the tidal pool," Michael gasped, his arms waving above his head to grab the attention of the men. "Bring the nets and lines."

Within minutes the fishermen gathered and within an hour, the entire villages of Cloghane, Brandon and Ballygwen were at the inlet. Some of the men struggled to tie lines around the dorsal fins of the smaller porpoises and tried to pull them out to deeper water. Others attempted to roll the huge adult porpoises into nets only to have the nets shred from the excessive weight. Everyone tried to help but the mere size of the mammals and the large number of them, between eighty and one hundred, made it an impossible task. After many failed attempts, the men reassembled and decided to concentrate their efforts on the porpoises furthest out from shore.

"Maybe we can save a few," said Michael's father.

"Have the lads fetch buckets of water from the sea and wet down the skins."

The people of the village had a great respect for the sea and all of its creatures. Their lives were bound to nature. They would do their best to save these magnificent creatures.

As the evening wore on, the full moon created strange shadows on the strand while the villagers continued to work. When the tide reached the point where it would start to begin its rise again, the useless work was abandoned. They had saved only a few but they could do no more. If some were still alive when the tide came up, perhaps they would be able to swim again.

After much discussion, it was decided to gut the fish that were too high on the sand for the tide to reach them. The fish would be cooked and used for food. What could not be consumed shortly would be smoked and stored for the winter. They needed to work quickly before the morning sun would beat down on the carcasses spoiling the food supply.

Some of the men built a fire on the beach to provide light and the women used the fire to boil tea water for the workers. No one slept that night.

They worked mostly in family groups with single men helping families with no men at all. It was a difficult task. Although the mammal skin cut easily enough, the size of the porpoises made sectioning difficult. The villagers tried to separate the fat for oil while determining which part of the meat to save.

Only six years earlier, like the rest of Ireland, the village had been starving. They lost more than half of the village population to hunger. Some died in their beds. Others died alongside of the road, crawling for help, which only showed how the hunger had affected the brain, for there was no help and everyone knew it. Some died in the government workhouses, on the other side of Connor Pass, near Dingle. Almost all of the starving died with green mouths, for in their desperation they had taken to eating grass.

It was not a surprise then, when one of the women began to call out in a loud voice to everyone who would listen, "The porpoises are a sign from God that we should have food. Sure, isn't it like manna from heaven, just like God sent to his people in the desert? Praise be to God, his Mother and all the Saints! We will have food this winter." The woman's words rang through the night air, followed by silence, as the images of sad memories swept over the assembled crowd. The work continued for several days.

Beached Porpoises (bhc)
Cloghane

Lisnakloween
Twenty-Four Years Later
Fall 1878

The young boy who found the porpoises in the tidal pool matured into a strong fisherman. He married Mary Murphy and since they were both from Lisnakloween, they built their stone cottage there on the ragged cliffs and together set about raising a flock of six. "Lis," as the locals called it, was a collection of cottages perched high above the shoreline with a view of the ocean that stretched for miles. The land on the mountainside was mostly rock and shale so farming was limited to a few potatoes and owning a handful of sheep that roamed the surrounding hills.

Aside from the hardy folk and the sheep, only the seagulls and fulmars ventured up to the heights of Lis. In winter, the wind howled around the hills while the turf fires warmed the spirit. When the fog and mist settled in, Lis was lost in the clouds to the villages of Brandon and Ballygwen hugging the shoreline below.

But springtime and summer in Lis were like nowhere else on earth. The sun coaxed out the wildflowers, the sea sent up fragrant breezes from below and the ocean shimmered with flashes of silver. It was easy to forget the hardships of winter.

The farms below Lis were tiny and resembled a patchwork quilt with stone walls dividing the spaces and setting the boundaries. Fathers divided their land into shares amongst their sons, who had later subdivided for their sons. Unable to break this cycle, they felt fortunate to have anything after the "Great Hunger." They used their small patch of earth to grow cabbage, spuds, maybe turnips. A few hens for eggs, a chicken for Sunday dinner and a pig butchered once a year rounded out the diet. Those families with nets or a boat enjoyed ocean treats like salmon, mackerel, herring and crabs. A farmer rich enough to own a cow could barter milk with neighbors.

There were no shops in Lis. The families who settled in Lis were self-reliant and independent. Each morning before dawn, Michael Fitzgerald hiked down the twisty, narrow trail to join the fishing fleet out of Brandon. Several hours later, his children would make the trek to school in Ballygwen.

On this day, the curragh rocked gently in the slow rolling waves as the dawn changed to morning. The two fishermen on board, Michael Fitzgerald and his brother worked side by side. Their family had always worked the nets. Mikeen, his name in Irish and his brother, Owen, learned from their father and his father before him. For fishermen like Mikeen and Owen, the market prices of herring ruled their economy. When the herring prices dropped, the village suffered. Likewise, a good price per pound meant happier times.

The two men were scooping the herring into four large baskets in the center of the small boat. They spent the last several hours shouting directions to each other and pulling the large, fish-laden nets into the boat. The herring was plentiful in the cold waters of the Atlantic and the schools of fish were easy to spot. The fisherman would watch for swooping, diving seagulls feasting on the fish. Then, they would row the curragh into the center of the activity checking for flashes of blue-green and silver, the telltale colors of herring. The fish, swimming close together by the thousands, just beneath the surface, were an easy target. With the net over the starboard side, one man would row in a clockwise circle, opposite to the direction of the swimming herring, and the fish would fill the nets. The second man needed to hang precariously over the side of the curragh to assure that the nets remained in an open position. Then, with a coordinated effort, they would haul the catch on board. For the men, the trick was balancing the curragh, the net and themselves. If one side of the net dropped lower than the other, the entire catch could be lost.

Today, the nets had lifted easily. There was no wind, and the brothers with fifty years of fishing experience between them, moved swiftly. The only remaining chores were to load the baskets, roll up the nets, and row back to the village pier.

Before they rowed back, the men settled into their morning ritual of a smoke and a chat. A light mist, heavy fog, or even a sea of white caps did not cancel the routine.

Mikeen offered his brother a cigarette. It was his turn. Tomorrow the offer would be returned. It was all part of the ritual. He cupped his reddened, callused fingers around the match to protect the flame and inhaled the first drag of the day. The muscled shoulders visibly relaxed and the two strong backs settled into a slouch.

Mikeen removed his cap and ran his fingers through the mass of red curls on his head. He lifted his weather-beaten face into the sun, checked the clouds, the wind direction and the waves. He replaced his cap, took a second drag on the fag and smiled at his brother.

"The good weather will last another day."

"'Twill, I'd say."

"This herring catch should bring a fair price."

"Aye," answered Owen.

They sat quietly. The water slapped the sides of the curragh in a steady rhythm. They enjoyed the sunshine, the cigarettes, the rocking, and each other's company. Owen broke the silence.

"I've been thinking about this notion of switching to the mackerel. We'll need new nets and have to drift farther out to sea."

Mikeen answered, slowly and thoughtfully, "'twill double the risk but could double the wage. Sure, we need to sleep on the decision a bit longer."

"Aye," responded Owen with a nod of his head.

The silence resumed. A few more puffs and they were finished with the fags. They flicked the butt ends into the waves and assumed their positions at the oars. In less than a minute, they were underway to the Brandon pier and the waiting market.

Mary Murphy worried about her husband, Mikeen, as he worked the ocean everyday. There was no such thing as a day off. If the herring were running, the men were working. She had knit him a cap and then colored it with the brightest red dye she could make from the roots of bushes on the mountain. Mikeen had liked the gift and called it his "lucky cap." From her perch high on the hill in Lis, Mary could spot Mikeen with the flash of red on the blue ocean.

Mary also had a wonderful spot for watching the weather as it rolled in from a distance across the Atlantic or if clouds approaching the mountains from the east should suddenly become threatening. Even so, she worried. So many men were lost over the years. Sudden storms, severe wind, unexpected tide rips, all could overturn the small curraghs.

The fishermen wore hand knit sweaters made from the wool of their mountain sheep. Each fishing village had its own pattern of stitches. Strangers could identify a man's home village by his sweater, regardless if he was in the pub or found lifeless washed upon the shore.

Mary knew all this, but when she married Mikeen she had accepted that fishing was his life and so it was hers. She prayed daily not to be a fisherman's widow.

Brandon Fishermen in Curragh (bhc)

Lis
June 1879 to 1889

Everywhere people went in the village, the talk was of mackerel and the proposed rail line between Castlegregory and Tralee. The men spoke of nothing else at the pub. The women gathered in groups near the shop. The crowd buzzed outside the chapel on Sunday mornings. People talked over tea, at the post office and in front of their fires in the evening. Mikeen and Mary decided they would be part of the new future and together with Owen, purchased mackerel nets.

Mackerel was going to change the villages of Brandon, Cloghane and Lis. The wheels of prosperity were finally beginning to turn; slowly but, there was movement. With some luck, there would be momentum.

Word spread of the initial success with the mackerel fishing and the number of men and fishing curraghs increased by the hundreds. Mikeen and Owen suddenly had an added burden. Inexperienced men were asking them for advice about the fishing.

"Did you meet the two men from Limerick?" Owen asked Mikeen one morning.

"Aye. A sorry lot, those two."

"I told them what they needed to know, but I fear for their safety. Telling them how to fish and doing it, are two different things altogether. They haven't a clue what's required and no idea of the danger on the water," complained Owen.

"I suppose they are desperate for success like the rest of us. But when they watch us do the job, it looks easy. They don't realize how many years we're doing it," answered Mikeen.

Shaking his head from side to side, Owen continued. "I don't want their blood on my hands when they drag them from the sea someday."

"Sure, you help where you can Owen, the rest is in God's hands. You can't be takin' on the whole group of newcomers. When the new pier in Brandon is finished next month, there will be even more men and boats comin', sure there will."

The daily mackerel catch created jobs for the women and children. The fish were gutted, salted and packed into barrels for transport. They built a drying shed in Brandon and the barrels moved to Tralee by donkey and cart. The only part of the plan to be completed was the railroad spur from Tralee to Castlegregory. In the meantime, there was work and prosperity for everyone.

Transporting mackerel from Brandon to Castlegregory (bhc)

Lis
June 1890

Unbeknownst to Mikeen and his family, all their good fortune with the mackerel fleet was soon to be defeated. There was an enemy advancing. It sneaked into the village and hid in the hay field. It lazed in the sun gathering strength before the attack. In May 1890, the first death occurred. A small child died of a high fever, but no one recognized the typhus. When the child's mother and two brothers fell within the week, panic spread.

Mikeen's fever started on a Thursday. It took thirteen days for the painful fever to run its course on the strong fisherman's body. Mary tended him with gentleness, all the time fighting the fearful thoughts inside her. If they both died, at least the children were grown. What if she lost the children? How could she go on everyday without them, without Mikeen? The questions tumbled around with the fear in her heart. She prayed the rosary continuously, like a mantra, that would keep her sane, as long as she did not stop. It was all she could do and she needed to do something. She needed to keep strong.

On the morning of June 4, 1890, burning with fever, covered with the telltale rash and with his mind lost in a typhoid stupor, Mikeen struggled to breathe. The doctor came, but by noon the struggle was ended. This strong fisherman, filled with hope for the future, a survivor of the Great Hunger, a brother, a husband and a father of six, was robbed of his destiny by the bite of a tick.

They laid him to rest in the cemetery attached to the old Church of Ireland, at the western end of Cloghane village. The cemetery sits high on a hill and from here you can see the inlet and the tidal pool where the young boy, Mikeen, had spotted the porpoises many years before. Mikeen would be pleased with the look of it.

Lis
Spring 1892

The rail line from Tralee to Castlegregory opened in 1891 to a great deal of excitement. The carts took the barrels to the waiting boxcars at the Castlegregory station. From the Tralee shipyards, they exported to the waiting markets in England and the USA.

The rail line transformed market days in Castlegregory. Instead of quiet streets, there was the hustle of passengers coming and going. A line of donkeys brought the mackerel barrels for loading. Cattle, sheep and pigs were hustled down the road to the station and the waiting boxcars. Supplies, tools and shop items were arriving to be unloaded. It was a hectic scene.

Owen continued fishing for mackerel. He joined up with a childhood friend but his fishing days were never the same without Mikeen. Mary, also distressed over losing Mikeen, focused all her attention on the children. The two middle girls, Johanna and Norah were anxious to follow a friend to America. For over a year now, they had been saving money for their passage.

Joan and Nan, as everyone called them, were inseparable. The young women were excited about the voyage. It was difficult on Mary. She knew it was the right decision but that didn't lessen the pain. She hid her sorrow and did her best to enter the planning with a smile. She spoke words of encouragement and helped to pack the cases. The leaving would be painful.

Holyoke, Massachusetts, USA
1892

Holyoke was a boomtown when the two young sisters arrived. Many of the young in the bustling city were immigrants. The paper mills were the predominant industry of the time but the mills devoured humanity as well as the logs. It churned people and pulp all in the name of profit. The east was growing and the need for lumber, paper supplies and pulp products was insatiable.

Nan and Joan found jobs in a hospital that repaired the bodies injured in the dangerous industry. Besides paying a salary, the hospital provided a dormitory for staff and three meals a day. The sisters moved in, learned their jobs, made friends and settled into a routine. Life was good.

Several months passed when Joan heard of a family looking for a cook and a maid. She hurried back to the dorm to tell her sister.

"I'm not sure we should leave the hospital," replied Nan with doubt in her voice.

"We'll make more money and have more time to ourselves," reasoned Joan. "Besides, if it doesn't work out, we can always come back to the hospital. What do you say, Nan?"

"Let's give it a try!"

Estate of Arthur and Dorothy Fielding, Holyoke

Arthur Fielding made his fortune during the development of the railroads. He and his wife, Dorothy, were a generous couple with five children. When the two Fitzgerald women came for their interview with Mrs. Fielding, James, the youngest Fielding child, had been with his mother. Mrs. Fielding was impressed with the way James responded to Nan and decided on the spot that the two sisters would be a wonderful asset to her household.

Nan was hired as the all around housekeeper, responsible for the front parlor, receiving visitors, serving the tea and sometimes supervising the children when their parents went away for social weekends. Joan was the cook and responsible for all the meals in the household. The Fieldings were proud of the two new employees. It did not take long for the reputation of Joan's fine Sunday dinners to travel around the small community of Holyoke. All of the Fielding's visitors left the estate spreading the word of the fine meals they had enjoyed and the warm reception they had received at the door. Mr. Fielding especially liked that his prominence in the town was enhanced. He was a man determined to be not only rich, but also influential. As far as Nan and Joan were concerned, the estate was a wonderful place to live and each month there were some extra dollars to send home to Kerry.

Joan had a gift for sewing. Without lessons, she had mastered intricate techniques with a needle. On their days off, Joan and Nan would travel into the city center and spend hours choosing bolts of cloth to make new dresses. They would negotiate with the clerk to give them half of one bolt and half of another for the price of one.

"How can we both wear the same dress?" they would explain to the clerk and the clerk unable to deal with the double team would sell them the cloth at half price. Then, in the evenings, when the Fielding children were in bed and dinner completed for the night, Nan would design and Joan would sew their latest creations.

For the many Irish men and women working in Holyoke, Sunday mass was the social gathering of the week. The well-dressed sisters were the fashion envy of the other young women. They would meet their friends on the way out of the cathedral and while chatting on the steps, make plans for their one weekday off duty. On these days, they would travel north by train to Boston or east to Newport. It was a wonderful year of travel for the two sisters.

Throughout these months, the sisters were faithful about sending money to Lis. For the first time in years, there was money for fruit or bread from the shop. Most important, it made all the difference for Mother and their four brothers and sisters at St. Brendan's Chapel in Cloghane. It was the custom of the time for the local priest to read the list of families who had not contributed a shilling that month. It was a humiliating experience to hear your name bellowed from the pulpit, feel your neighbors disapproving stares, and hear the whispered secrets of shame. This cruel instrument of social pressure was used to provide an annual income for repair of the chapel and support of its priest. Now that her daughters faithfully sent the shilling, the family walked proudly each week.

Norah and Johanna Fitzgerald
Holyoke, Massachusetts, circa 1894

Lis
February 1896

Mary's cottage was in a tizzy these days. Her oldest and her youngest daughters were getting married and on the same day! A double wedding!

Mane, the oldest, aged twenty-eight was engaged to Michael Lenihan from Brandon Quay. Jane, twenty-one, was engaged to Patrick Rourke. The wedding would be in St. Brendan's Chapel in Cloghane with the three families attending.

The February weather was cold and nasty but the two sisters never noticed. The wedding was scheduled for Saturday, February 3, and following the ceremony, the families agreed to have sandwiches and two cakes, one for each bride and groom. They planned to celebrate at the Shea's pub located at the Brandon T road. Mother volunteered to make both the wedding cakes and she was busy for weeks.

News of all the excitement reached Joan and Nan by letter in Holyoke.

"It's times like these, I wish I could just skip off and be home," sighed Joan.

"A double wedding! What a special event it 'twill be," responded Nan.

"'Tis too bad father did not live to see it. Sure he would be popping his buttons with pride that day. And Mam making two wedding cakes. She must be exhausted altogether."

Suddenly, Joan perked up with enthusiasm. "Let's go to the shops and see if we can find something grand to send to each couple."

"Wonderful idea. Just give me a minute to get me hat." In less than five minutes, Nan and Joan were on their way.

Ten months later, Mane and Michael Lenihan were blessed with a son and they named him Michael. He was the first grandchild for Mary and she was excited and grateful to God for the new blessing. Four months later, Jane and Patrick Rourke had Michael Patrick. Mary was thrilled and often repeated, "A double wedding and a double blessing of grandsons named Michael."

The following year Jane gave birth to John Francis but he died within a few months. Jane's third son, Joseph, was born June 11, 1899 and helped Jane to deal with the loss of wee Johnny.

The months of 1899 were ticking by as everyone prepared for the coming of 1900 and a new century. William decided to try his future in America leaving only "Ned" (Edward) at home with his mother, Mary. Suddenly, the overflowing cottage was quiet.

But the new century brought more sorrow to the Fitzgeralds. The winter was exceptionally cold with tremendous amounts of rain making it difficult to keep the cottages warm and the bedding dry. Many suffered with the flu. The only remedy available was a hot toddy and bed rest, but it was not enough for Jane. She died of lung complications brought on by the flu on May 5, 1900. She was twenty-five. Patrick Rourke was left alone to raise his two sons, Michael and Joseph.

Mary was distressed with the loss of her daughter, Jane, and struggled against the odds, to regain her strength.

Holyoke
June 1900

One Tuesday morning in late June, as the sisters finished their routine chores at the Fieldings, they headed towards the kitchen for a cup of tea. Jim, the family chauffeur, called out to them.

"Just got back from the post office. Letter from home for you. I left it on the cupboard in the kitchen."

The girls smiled and hurried into the kitchen expecting news from Mam. To their surprise, this letter was not a handwriting they recognized. Nan opened the letter.

"It's from Mane. Sure I should have known her writing."

Joan replied, "You can read it first, while I pour the tea." She turned and reached into the cabinet choosing two china cups with matching saucers when she heard a loud thump behind her. She turned to see Nan collapsed on the floor. Joan rushed to her and knelt down.

"What's wrong? Here, let me help you to a chair."

Nan was sobbing and as limp as a rag doll. It was then that Joan picked up the crumpled letter and began to read it herself.

"Oh God, no, not Jane, not our little sister!"

When Jim returned to the kitchen, he was shocked to find the two sisters sobbing and rocking in each other's arms.

Dorothy Fielding was preparing the menu for next week's dinner party when she heard the knock on her study door.

"Come in," she called out quickly, expecting one of her children, since Arthur was away on business until tomorrow.

The door opened slowly as Joan entered the beautifully appointed room. She walked across the Persian carpet to stand in front of the desk. Mrs. Fielding rose and with a gracious sweep of her arm directed Joan to one of the Chippendale chairs as she came around the desk and sat in a matching chair next to Joan. Dorothy knew this was important for Joan to interrupt her and she sensed from Joan's demeanor that she needed to listen attentively. Mrs. Fielding sat and waited for Joan to speak.

"I don't know where to begin except to say that Nan and I must be leaving. I do not have a date yet but I thought you should know, to give you time to find a replacement. We have been very happy here with you and your family and I want to thank you for all your kindness."

Dorothy wanted to help Joan but she did not want to cross the line and invade her privacy. If Joan should share her story, then Dorothy would feel comfortable about the situation. She thought about other young women who had worked for her. One had found herself pregnant and another was just too homesick to stay. But, Joan was a strong individual with a sense of loyalty, and she was not afraid to try new things or meet new people. Dorothy couldn't imagine what was serious enough to cause Joan's departure.

"What's happened, Joan?" asked Mrs. Fielding.

Joan related her story, explaining the letter from Mane with the news of her sister, Jane, and now, Mam's illness. Going home was the only solution that made sense to her. She told Mrs. Fielding about Jane's sons, a toddler and an infant.

"We need to be home," ended Joan.

Mrs. Fielding was upset for Joan and Nan. She could not sit while thinking about the situation. She rose from her chair and started to pace the room while Joan continued with the details. She loved Nan and Joan as if they were her own daughters. She understood the dilemma and simply nodded to show that she heard and understood.

When Joan got up to leave the room, Mrs. Fielding said quietly, "I will find another cook and another housekeeper, but I will never find a replacement for the two of you in my heart. If you ever need anything in the future, I will be here for you."

A replacement was quickly found for Nan's position but not for Joan's. The sisters decided Nan should leave and Joan would follow as soon as possible. When Nan arrived home, she took over the care of Mam while her sister, Mane, helped Patrick Rourke with the two little ones. Four months later, Mam succumbed to influenza on New Year's Eve, December 31, 1900.

Lis
Spring 1901

Joan's return to Cloghane was difficult. There was no one to meet her at the ship, so she continued on her own to the village. As she approached, she thought about the contrast between Lis and the Fielding home, with all its antiques and expensive furnishings.

As the pony and trap rounded the bend in the road, it was like seeing the place for the first time, as if she wore a new pair of spectacles. How small, how beautiful, this tiny village. The beauty of the place made her heart sing and she began to whistle. Nan, who had been baking in anticipation of the homecoming, heard the familiar tune and realized Joan was coming up the path. She dropped what she was about and ran out of the cottage.

Everyone was thrilled to see Joan and rejoiced at having her home. The neighbors stopped by, some alone and some in small groups. Within two weeks, there had been three coelis with music, dancing and song. For the first time since Jane and Mother's deaths, the cottage heard laughter. The Fitzgerald clan began to feel like a family again.

Village of Cloghane
Summer 1903

Saturday was Pattern Day and the entire countryside was out for the festivities. Joan met Nan and her husband Dan Moriarity at the crossroads just outside Cloghane village. Nan and Danny had married in February 1902 and settled on the Moriarity farm in Cappeagh.

The weather was cooperating today and many vendors had set up tables alongside the road. The most popular treat on Pattern Day was Dingle Pie. Since it was early in the day, they decided to wait before settling down to a feast. As they walked they kept a mental note of which booth appeared to have the pies with the most mutton and the richest looking soup. They all agreed that the corner booth was where they would return.

As they entered the village, they could hear the children shouting in a field off to the right so they headed in that direction first. Sure enough, the races had begun and the children were cheering for friends. They met some friends from

Brandon and another who was preparing to leave for the States shortly. As they passed a group of young men, Nan spotted Thomas Finn, a cousin from Ballygwen. Joan and Tom had not seen each other in years, so it was Nan who started the conversation.

"How are ye lad? Haven't seen your face in so long, I thought you must be lost to us altogether."

"Did you not hear that I was in Limerick, working?"

"Not at 'tall. We've seen your brother, sure he never mentioned Limerick."

"Tom, do you remember my sister, Joan? She was in the states last time you were up to Lis."

"We haven't seen each other since we were children. Didn't know I had such a fine lookin' woman for a cousin," he teased.

"Oh, the Blarney will get you everywhere," replied Joan with a laugh. "Easy telling you're a cousin all right."

"Are ye stayin' for the music?" inquired Tom. "This group is from Dingle and said to be the best around. They start playing at four o'clock."

"Aye, sure music is why we've come," answered Joan.

"Don't be forgettin' the Dingle pies," interrupted Danny. "Why don't you join us for the feast, Tom? And then we'll be together for the music."

"Just let me say good bye to the lads inside here and then I'll be along." He turned and ran into the pub.

The Dingle pies were as good as the memories from last year. Everyone had two and Tom was able to muster up three. They finished up the meal with a porter just as the musicians started.

The music was what the crowd needed to enter into the festivities with full gusto. There were group sing alongs, ballads by individuals, some fine step dancing and of course, a few requests to round out the evening. It was a very late night.

Three months went by before Joan met her cousin, Thomas, again. She had made the long walk down from Lis to get to the postal window in the shop at Brandon. Thomas spoke first.

"Joan, 'tis great to see you again. How is yer day?"

"I'm grand, Thomas."

"Are ye by any chance friends with Eileen Rowan from Lis?"

"Aye, she's a neighbor of mine."

"We're goin' with four others to the football game, next Sunday week. Want to come along? You'll have company on that walk down the mountain."

"Is that the game against the lads from Mayo?"

"Aye, the very same."

"Then count me in. I love a good match."

"We're meeting' at the crossroads, one o'clock. See you there. Regards to Nan and the family." He tipped his cap to her as he waved goodbye and stepped out into the misty rain.

Eileen and Joan arrived a little early at the crossroads on Sunday. While they were waiting for the others to arrive, Eileen started a conversation about Thomas.

"Sure, I didn't know he was your cousin."

"Well, we haven't seen much of each other since we were young ones playing around the curraghs."

"I think he's beautiful with those big blue eyes and black hair. And when he tilts his head to give you a smile, me heart goes faint."

"Oh, he's a looker all right. No good to me though, he's me cousin."

"Promise me you won't tell what I've said," pleaded Eileen.

"Your secret is safe," Joan assured her.

Ballygwen Village

Thomas Finn was a shoemaker by trade, taught by his father, Michael. He did not have a shop; instead, neighbors dropped any repair work they had at his family's cottage. His tools were few but essential. If a new pair of shoes were needed, he would trace the customer's feet, make a pattern, and cut the leather from prepared hides he had purchased in Tralee. The stitching was important in a new shoe. The best leather in the world would deteriorate quickly if the stitches were not secure. Thomas apprenticed with his father and in Limerick to get his stitches perfect.

Thomas was well liked in the village of Ballygwen. He was the friendly sort, always with a story, always with a joke and a warm welcome. He was popular in the pub where he was known to burst into a song with very little prodding. The women enjoyed his warm personality and good looks while the men enjoyed his conversation. Everyone was pleased to see him home from Limerick.

The leatherwork was sporadic because it was tied to the seasons, the crops and the fishing. When the crops were harvested and the farmers had money from the markets, they would line up the family for new shoes. Not that it meant everyone got new shoes. Older children passed their old ones down to the next in line but Thomas would repair worn soles, add a dab of polish and the youngsters were happy.

In the summer, the children wore no shoes, but the opening of school brought a flurry of business to his cottage door. It became quiet again until the Christmas season. Old Wellington's were a source of irritation. They were patched the same as a bicycle tube. The Wellies were worn in the muddy fields and wet grasses, exactly what they were designed for, but exactly what caused the patches to open again. Thomas pondered this repair method often and hoped to one-day find glue that could withstand moisture or maybe design an alternative method of repair. His mother told him he was a dreamer.

"Thomas, be content with your lot in life, son. Sure haven't we been lucky enough to survive the famine and the cold winters. You are from strong stock boy, don't forget it. People will always be needing the shoes, so you will have your work. Your father and I are proud of you, and we're asking no more."

"Aye, ma. Yet it would be nice to have a few extra shillings to buy a pony or maybe rent a field and put a few cattle on it."

"Thomas, you are a dreamer," was her standard reply.

During the weeks that the work was slow, Thomas visited Eileen and Joan on the mountain in Lis. The three of them had wonderful times. Weather permitting, they would go hiking, if not, they spent hours around the fire. Thomas would ask Joan to tell stories of Holyoke and the ship she had traveled on, the GERMANIC. He would tell the girls about Limerick and funny tales of tricks the apprentices played. Eileen would play the concertina while Thomas played the harmonica and Joan would sing.

Thomas always felt refreshed when he walked down the mountain and home to Ballygwen. His step was lighter and the road seemed shorter. On this day, he realized he was falling in love with Joan, not Eileen.

"I must stop this feeling inside me. Nothing good can come of it. I'll stay away for awhile, and let this feeling pass."

Lately, Joan was having trouble sleeping. Her mind kept going back to the evening she was alone with Thomas in front of the fire in her cottage. She had felt the desire to lean over and kiss him. She imagined how soft and warm he would be to her touch. She fantasized that he would kiss her back with passion and whisper wonderful words of love in her ear. She tossed and tumbled to rid her mind of such thoughts and hasten the return of sleep.

When Thomas was not seen on the mountain for a month, Eileen used her brother's shoes as an excuse to go to Ballygwen. Thomas saw her approaching and went down the lane to meet her.

Eileen was pleased to have the chance to speak to him beyond the earshot of other adults.

"Thomas, I've missed you. You haven't been to Lis in a month. Did I do something to make you angry and keep you away?"

"No, not a'tall." He took the shoes from her arm and examined both sides of them as they walked. He was having difficulty finding the right words and he hoped playing with the shoes would give him some time to think.

"Were you planning to come back again?" she asked.

"Sure, I've just been busy, is all." He tried to sound convincing. Once or twice, he had thought about what to say, but it was going to be when he was ready, when he would go to Lis. Her coming to Ballygwen had taken him by surprise.

He continued, "I thought maybe I was giving you the wrong impression by coming so often. I thought me intentions could be confusing. I didn't want to hurt anyone, so I just stayed away. I suppose I should have told you."

Eileen answered softly, "I asked Joan if she knew why you weren't coming and she just shook her head. I think she misses you too."

At the mention of Joan, his neck started to blush and he hoped that Eileen wouldn't notice his sweaty palms. "I saw her at church Sunday last. Did she not tell you?"

"That's not what I mean, Thomas. The three of us had such wonderful times. We can't understand what's happened. I thought you and I had something special but I guess I was mistaken."

"Well, let's go inside and see what we can do with this pair of shoes. When me work is caught up, I'll come to Lis again and we'll have another music session."

He was relieved when she finally left. What a mess I have created, he thought to himself.

The Fish Market, Brandon Pier

Every Thursday morning Joan would walk down the mountain to meet Nan at the intersection of the Lis road and the road to Brandon. Nan would travel from Cappeagh on the pony and cart, pick up Joan and together head to the pier to purchase fish from the local catch. This weekly shopping expedition was a way for the two sisters to visit and keep in touch. This day, Joan was bursting to talk. She needed advice and there was no one in the world she trusted more than Nan.

"Nan, remember the day we were in Holyoke and you received the letter from Danny?"

"Aye, who could forget, it changed everything."

"Tell me, how did you know Danny was the one for you?"

"Where is this going?"

"I'll explain, but I need to know how a woman can be sure about a man."

"Well now, if I knew that, I'd know one of the secrets of the universe. I think it is different for each person. Now tell me what's goin' on for ye to be asking me these questions."

Joan told Nan the whole story of Thomas visiting her and Eileen in Lis, about the great times they shared and how the romance had blossomed between herself and Thomas instead of Eileen and Thomas.

Nan nodded at her sister, "I can't say that I'm surprised. The two of you are well matched. You seem to fit together nicely."

Joan was distressed when she answered. "Nan, he is me cousin. We can never marry."

"Sure you can, he is only your second cousin."

"What are you talking about, Nan? We were always taught cousins couldn't marry."

"Aye, true enough but then they made that announcement in church."

"What announcement?" asked Joan, holding her breath for the answer.

"Don't you remember? Let me think for a moment. I will bet you were still in Holyoke and Thomas was in Limerick. Maybe the two of you never heard." Nan paused to take a breath and before she could continue, Joan interrupted her.

"Heard what?"

"It was announced, one Sunday, because of The Great Hunger and the population loss. The Church was looking favorably upon requests for dispensations to marry cousins. Each case would be handled individually, but couples were encouraged to apply."

"Oh, my God, I've never heard this before." Joan held her hands up to her temples trying to concentrate on Nan's words.

Nan asked her gently, "Are you two serious enough for that step?"

Joan started to sob with tears of relief and nodded her head.

February 1904

Johanna Fitzgerald and Thomas Finn received their dispensation. They married in St. Brendan's chapel in Cloghane on Saturday, the thirteenth day of February. Joan's brother Ned and her sisters Nan and Mane were there as well as the Finn family.

Thomas had a sister named Julia, married to John Dunne, a harness maker in Castlegregory. The Dunne cottage was on Forge Road and it was arranged to have the wedding celebration there.

In preparation for the marriage, Thomas found a local man in Ballygwen who leased him a field at the rate of one half crown per year. It was a tiny plot measuring approximately fifty feet by fifty feet, but it was large enough for a cottage and a tiny garden. This plot fronted on the road passing through Ballygwen. Only a few hundred yards south of the field was a fresh water spring that flowed from the mountain near Lis. The white strand and blue Atlantic was a short walk to the west. They decided it would be a fine start. Living in Ballygwen was going to be a luxury for Joan who no longer had to trek up the mountain road to Lis.

Thomas started to build the cottage and with help from his father, brothers and uncles, it moved along. The progress was slow. Thomas was used to working with small needles and awls to make shoes. This job required him to move heavy beams and stones. His body would ache by the end of the day but the next morning, he was up and ready to have another go at it. He knew the neighbors were watching and wondering would he ever finish, but there was no doubt for him and Joan. She helped him wherever she could and kept him fed during the long days. Eventually, it was finished and they moved in for summer.

Thomas was doing well with the shoe trade and his brother Patrick had opened a shop, near the Cappeagh crossroad with his wife, Catherine Moriarity. If money was scarce between shoe jobs, Joan and Thomas could buy at the shop and pay the debt when the shoe season was busy again.

They were married just over a year when the first bundle of joy arrived at their cottage. Born on St. Patrick's Day, 17th of March, 1905, they christened her Mary Cecilia, for Joan's mother. It wasn't long until little Mary Cecilia was walking and talking. Thomas made her first pair of shoes and the small family was content with life in Ballygwen.

Two years after Mary's birth, their first son was born on July 3, 1907. They named him Michael after his two grandfathers.

One evening, as Thomas sat by the fire, he began to think aloud. "Aren't we blessed with a girl and a boy."

"It is truly a blessing. Moreover, a double blessing to us who had such a late start in marriage. Our babies are beautiful altogether. To think we almost didn't marry. Sure we mortals never know what God's plan is for us."

"Truer words were never spoken."

Ballygwen
Springtime 1913

Sundays were a special day of the week when the family would walk to Mass in Cloghane, a distance of two miles from Ballygwen.

The children were able to handle the walk. They were used to walking everywhere and there were many distractions along the way. Now there were four children. Mary Cecilia was seven, Mikeen was five and Patrick was three. If Patrick tired along the way, Thomas carried him on his shoulders. Joan left baby Owen, three months old, with a neighbor. They would meet up with Nan and Danny at the Cappeagh crossroad. Joan's children loved meeting up with Nan's son, Thomas, who was nine.

It rained often, when the clouds moved in off the ocean and dropped moisture on the side of Mount Brandon. On these mornings, Danny hitched the pony and cart and everyone piled into it. If the day was fine, they walked together for the last quarter mile.

Mane's family also had grown. She had four children: Malachi, John, Nancy and Joan. In addition, there were Jane's two sons and Ned's son and daughter, to bring the total number of cousins at the chapel each Sunday to thirteen. It was a chatty group as the adults exited the Chapel and gathered to chat and the children played with the warning, "Don't abuse your Sunday best."

Dinner was served at noon each day, when the men came in from the fields and the children returned from the schoolhouse. But, Sunday dinner was special. Dessert was served. If fruit was available, Joan made a tart, if not, she made rice pudding. After dinner, it was the tradition to visit other families. During the football season, everyone gathered at the field or the local pub for a music coeli.

They lost Owen in May 1913. They were never sure what caused his death. The first flowers of the season had bloomed and the toddler was fascinated with the vivid colors. Just fifteen months old, he would walk from plant to plant, point with his tiny finger, and attempt to say, "flower." He was outside with Mary Cecilia and Patrick when he suddenly started to cry, grabbed at his throat and fell to the ground. Mary Cecilia ran quickly for Mam.

"Mam, Mam, it's Owen. Come quick!"

Joan was busy counting potatoes on the table in preparation for dinner. She stopped and ran to her youngest son. Owen's face was already changing from bright red to blue. Joan knew immediately that Owen couldn't breathe. She tried putting her finger into the baby's throat and shouted for Mary to run for her father. Next Joan tried breathing into the baby's mouth, forcing air into his lungs. There was no response. She tried turning Owen over onto his stomach and put pressure on his lungs from behind. There was no response. She turned him onto his back and tried breathing into his mouth again. There was no response.

In just five minutes, Thomas came running along with three of the neighbor men. They saw the limp body in Joan's arms and knew they were too late.

When they bathed the little body for burial, they discovered the mark of a bee sting and they wondered could a bee have caused such damage? A neighbor man said he had heard of such a thing happening years ago. They buried Owen in the old cemetery, high on the hill in Cloghane, next to his grandparents, Mikeen and Mary and Aunt Jane.

Joan was feeling tired these days. It took her two months to believe she was pregnant. For some reason, based on nothing but a feeling, Joan did not think she would have any more children. This pregnancy was a surprise. Her fifth child, Thomas, named after his father, was born on July 14, 1914.

Life was getting more difficult for Joan and Thomas with each passing year. The cottage was small and cramped. There were six mouths to feed now instead of two, and the children needed clothing. Joan, always handy with a needle and thread since Holyoke, did her best to economize. She thought back to all the dresses she had made for herself and Nan in Holyoke. She would love to have just one of them now to make a darling dress for Mary Cecilia. The boys were easier to dress because they shared the clothing amongst them and often she got hand-me-downs from their male cousins, but Mary Cecilia was one of only three girls in the bunch.

Joan coaxed as many vegetables as she could from the sandy soil. Joan had more soil than she had in Lis, but fewer feet of it. She grew potatoes and veggies out back and where others had a border of flowers out front, she planted a row of cabbage. Anything to keep her family intact.

There was a fast moving stream nearby the cottage, but the folks in Ballygwen called it "the well." Its water was clear and cold from the mountain feeding it. It wound its way down the cliffs, past the National School at the foot of the mountain, then turned to pass behind the cluster of Ballygwen houses, and finally emptied into the Atlantic a quarter mile past the village.

Mary Cecilia and Mikeen, the two oldest children, were each responsible for filling a bucket with water and bringing it home every morning before school. Patrick, still too young to handle the heavy buckets, liked to tag along. The water was needed in the house for everything from washing hands and faces, to making soup, porridge and tea. A black kettle or cauldron was always simmering on the open hearth, ready at a moment's notice.

On a fine day, the well was a gathering place for the women who turned the laundry chore into a social gathering. There were several large rocks convenient for washing clothes. Using brown soap, the women scrubbed the clothing between their hands, beat it against the rocks to loosen heavy soil and then wrung as much water as possible. If the wind was calm, the wet clothing was draped on top of the bushes to dry in the sunshine. Later in the day it was gathered and carried home. This efficient method eliminated the need to carry heavy loads of wet clothing back to the cottage and peg it on a line. During the rainy season, the washing hung indoors in front of the hearth.

It was getting to be late summer, time to cut the hay and stack it in the fields to dry. One morning, Thomas called to his oldest son, Mikeen.

"Mikeen, I think you are strong enough this year to help with the thatch and learn the roping."

"Aye. 'Twould be great," responded Mikeen as he quickly finished his bread and tea.

"Can I go on the roof?"

"Aye. The men rotate the jobs and you will work alongside me." Mikeen's face broke into a broad smile. Patrick and Tomasin wanted to be included.

"Not yet, your turn will come soon enough."

"Then, can we come and watch?" questioned Patrick.

"Aye."

The men worked together in teams of three and moved around to repair each other's cottage. The man on the ground would pass the hay to the one on the ladder and he in turn would pass it to the worker on the roof. The children helped where they could and collected the rocks need for roof weights. Once the thatch was in place, a net of rope covered the roof and the rock weights secured the end of each rope. Villages close to the sea always added stones for protection from fierce winter storms off the Atlantic.

Johnny, one of Mikeen's friends, came by the Finn cottage asking his friend to walk the strand. When he heard that Mikeen was included in the thatching group, he was envious. He, too, wanted to watch and soon there were more spectators than workers on the narrow lane. It took over a week to repair just one roof and although Mikeen's father had given him work gloves, Mikeen's fingers were raw from knotting the bundles of hay and the roping on the roof. Mikeen never complained. He was elated to be included in the group and share the pride of a job completed.

Patrick, only seven, spent his summer days with the other children exploring the seashore, fishing or gathering seaweed to fertilize the planting beds. They collected periwinkles from the rocks near Cahir Point. Using a sharp stick the children scraped the periwinkles off the rocks and collected them in a bucket with seawater. At home, the delicacy was boiled in fresh water, removed from the shell and served in a stew. It was a treat not to be missed.

The women were busy also with the summer chores. This was the time to change all the bedding in the cottage. The mattress sacks were opened, the old hay discarded and fresh hay inserted to create new mattresses and pillows.

Mary was learning from Mam how to be sure the hay was ready for stuffing and how to check for field mites so as not to carry them into the house. They had collected empty flour sacks over the winter and now they washed them and stitched them together to form new sheets.

Thomas added a coat of whitewash to the walls and soon the cottage was clean and fresh, ready to begin another winter season of long evenings by the fire.

Every August, Mary Cecilia would accompany Mam on an outing to Tralee. They traveled with Nan and Mane on the pony and cart as far as Castlegregory where they boarded the train to the bustling city. They bought yard goods for sewing and maybe some trim. They window-shopped and one year, Mam bought a beautiful hat for Mary Cecilia.

"You are growing into a fine young lady," said Mam as the two faces looked into the mirror at the new hat. "You deserve a chance to dress like one. On the train ride home, I must tell you about the finery in Holyoke."

Before leaving Tralee, the women had a cup of tea and scones in a shop, then boarded the last train back to Castlegregory.

Mary Cecilia wanted to pinch herself to be sure she was not dreaming. She loved these outings more than her birthday, more than Christmas, more than anything. All year long, she was the only girl in the cottage but once a year, on this special day, she felt like the Queen of Ballygwen.

Of her three brothers, Mary Cecilia was closest to Mikeen. They were friends going to school, helped each other with lessons and looked out for each other in the village. Not that they did not look out for Paddy and Tomasin, but the ages separated them. Mikeen was her peer while the younger boys were her responsibility, as if she were the nanny. Plus, Mikeen kept a secret when needed and the feelings were reciprocated.

Mikeen's daily chore was to water and exercise the pony for his Uncle Dek. Every day, Tomasin went along with Mikeen, followed by their dog, Tiny. Tomasin and the dog were inseparable.

"Remember Tomasin, if you want to come along, keep the dog away from the pony. Don't spook him."

"I'll keep him with me, Mikeen. I promise." Everyday the dog would run ahead and create a commotion and Tomasin would run after the dog, calling over his shoulder to his brother, "I've got him!" Mikeen would laugh and enjoy the humor of the scene. He never did get angry with little Tomasin.

Paddy was the brother with the talent. He loved music and played any instrument by ear. He started with a tin whistle, then a flute, then a neighbor's concertina. Everyone said he had Aunt Jane's gift. She too was a wonder for the music and song. When Patrick Rourke, Jane's husband, heard Patrick play he decided to surprise his nephew. For Patrick's birthday, he gently wrapped Jane's concertina. From that day on, music flowed from Paddy to everything he touched.

St. Stephen's Day, the twenty-sixth of December, was a day of merriment that helped to continue the enjoyment of Christmas. The young folk of the village dressed in self-created costumes, with painted faces or masks. They played instruments, sang songs and otherwise entertained as best they could.

This year, Tomasin was old enough to participate and his older brother Paddy had agreed to take him along. They had worked on their costumes for several days now, binding small bundles of straw together to place around their backs or bellies to change their shape and maybe conceal their identity. Tomasin had an old hat from Uncle Dec and Paddy had a scarf from Mam for the final touch.

"Now you must learn the words to the song," said Paddy and he began to teach Tomasin the little verse.

"The wren, the wren, the king of all birds,
On St. Stephen's Day was caught in the furze,
And though he is little, his family is great,
So rise up landlady, and give us a treat."

"I don't really understand the words," sighed Tomasin.

"Not to worry, lad. If you learn them, you will feel a part of the group. The whole idea is for the people to give us a treat. If they don't, we will bury the wren across from their door and bad luck will be on that house for a year."

"Where will we get the wren?"

"Well, last year we had a real one because Tom O'Neil was lucky enough to catch one, under the hay pile. If we don't have a real one, we can make one from some cloth. 'Tis lots of fun. You will see."

"I remember when they came to our cottage last year. What a noise and commotion. I stood behind Da when they came."

"Aye. But look how big you have grown since last year. This time you will be making the noise outside. Agreed?"

"Aye. I can't wait."

When the day arrived, they traveled around with four other lads from school. Paddy, the best musician, played the concertina and led the songs. The other boys, with a tin whistle and spoons, were mostly noise backing up the musician.

Thomas and Patrick Finn circa 1926

One cottage gave them slices of Christmas cake and another gave them a penny to share. This caused a great deal of conversation as they decided to save it until the shop opened the next day, buy a treat, and split it six ways.

The most wonderful treat of the day was an orange slice for each lad. It came from an old woman that Tomasin didn't know because they had walked for miles and were now far from Ballygwen. He held the orange slice as if it were gold. He lifted it to his nose and enjoyed the aroma. He licked it with his tongue, tasted its sweetness. Then, he nibbled a small bite of the peel that surrounded the slice and enjoyed its texture. Somewhere in his memory, he was sure he had tasted an orange before, but he couldn't place the occasion. Finally, he bit into the slice and felt some juice run down his chin. It was the best treat of all.

By the time they returned to Ballygwen that evening, Tomasin's legs were tired and his feet sore from all the walking. Not that he minded, he wouldn't have missed it for anything. When they entered the cottage, his parents were waiting to hear all about his first St. Stephen's Day. Within half an hour, he was sound asleep in front of the fire.

"Paddy, thank you for taking him this year," said Mam. "He was so excited. He didn't interfere too much with you and your lads, did he?"

"Ah no, sure he was struggling to keep up but he never complained. We took a rest every now and then, but we needed it too. It was kind of fun to be teaching him the traditions. I'm getting kind of old meself to be doing this, so I wanted him to come along, before I give it up."

Da smiled, nodded, and taking a drag on his pipe added to the conversation, "It's not easy growing up. We need to leave some things behind to keep moving through life."

It was about this time that Thomas began to experience his "troubles" with the drink. It was hardly noticeable at first, staying at the pub too long after the Sunday football match or having just one more pint. It was contained to Sundays and many of Tom's mates seemed to do the same. He did not stand out.

Joan started to pay more attention after Mikeen came home from school one day with a torn shirt and blackened eye.

"What in the world has happened to you, lad? Are you hurt? Come here so I can wash that eye." Mikeen moved closer to his mother with caution. He didn't answer any of her questions.

"What happened to you, Mikeen?"

"Me and Johnny had a fight. Tha's all."

"Tell me what happened. You don't usually fight."

"It was nothing, Ma."

Just then, Mary Cecilia came into the cottage. Her mother turned to her and asked for information.

"Do you know what happened to your brother here?" Michael gave Mary a look that said, don't tell.

Mary looked at the floor, stalling to think of an excuse. "I wasn't there when it happened. I only heard about it."

"And what did you hear?"

"Only that Johnny and Mikeen had a real bloody battle in front of the school house and the teacher didn't see them until it was over. That's all."

Suddenly the cottage half door swung open and Patrick bounded in, breathless.

"Is it true you knocked Johnny's tooth out and gave him a bloody nose? The lads said you were fighting because Johnny called Da a bloody drunk. Is it true, Mikeen?"

There was total silence in the cottage. Young Patrick looked from face to face, expecting an answer.

Mary Cecilia would be the first of her generation to leave. She kept a stiff upper lip in front of everyone but inside her stomach was in knots. There wasn't any choice. She had been sitting in front of the fire two weeks earlier when she first heard the decision had been made for her. Mam had talked quietly and Mary Cecilia had cried. Her tears were salty and she could taste them in the corner of her mouth as she tried to object. It was obvious; unknown to Mary Cecilia, her mother had been planning this for quite some time. Saving a shilling here and hiding a pound there, Mam had amassed the cost of a one way voyage to the United States for Mary Cecilia. Mam saw it as the only way out for her oldest child, for the family.

Da had been drunk again last night. Lately, he was drunk more often than he was sober. Always drinking what little he had earned.

As a result, the family was often without necessities. Joan was out of patience with her husband, Thomas. He had squandered the house money for the last time. As far as she was concerned, the children would have to get out on their own. There was no future here in Ballygwen. She would save what she could and one by one, she would rescue them from this fate. Mary Cecilia was the oldest and the only daughter. She would be the first to go. Joan had written to the Fieldings in Holyoke. Since then, Joan's plans had been full steam ahead. It had taken her months to save the twenty pounds. She knew her husband, Thomas, would be angry when she told him, but she could live with that, just as she had been living with the drinking. Besides, she thought to herself, things couldn't be any worse.

Da's drinking, known as "the problem," would rear its ugly head every time he collected from his customers. He would take the money and travel to Tralee for his leather supplies. He never came home with supplies, only a hangover. He would sober up for a week or so, apologize up and down, and then call on all the Saints in Heaven to witness his intentions to never let it happen again.

Joan had tried sending the boys to Tralee with Da but their efforts to drag him from the pub were thwarted by his drinking buddies, who knew Thomas still had a few pounds in his pocket. Thomas would eventually come home and the cycle repeated itself.

In an effort to keep money away from Thomas, Joan would see a shoe customer in the village, and suggest they could pay her for the work, saving them the trip to her cottage. If they lived nearby, she would suggest they could pay their bill in chickens, eggs or vegetables.

Using these two techniques, she had managed to keep the family from the soup kitchen. Each month the margin of comfort narrowed and Joan felt like she was losing control. Her new plan for the children gave her a sense of purpose again.

Holyoke
January 1923

Mrs. Fielding's delight faded quickly. She had been thrilled to spot the Irish letter amongst the usual morning assortment of mail. But as she read the letter from Joan an overwhelming sadness settled in.

Joan's letter explained that she needed Mrs. Fielding's help and could her daughter, Mary Cecilia, work in the Fielding household? If not, perhaps they knew another distinguished family in need of domestic help. Mary Cecilia was a hard worker, quick to learn and Joan had personally taught her the etiquette and manners required for such a position. In addition, Joan had the money for Mary's passage.

Mrs. Fielding broke into a smile. "I'll bet you did teach her," she thought aloud as she reminisced about the happy days the two women had shared in the past. "I will discuss it this very evening with Arthur. I am sure we can add another pair of hands to the kitchen staff." Mary Cecilia would probably arrive in the spring, just in time for the summer entertaining. "It will be like family arriving!"

Delighted and with her decision made, she headed for the kitchen in search of Agnes, her household cook. She wanted Agnes involved in the planning so she would be sure to accept Mary Cecilia when she arrived. Keeping peace amongst the domestics in a household required foresight. Tension amongst the staff often resulted in an unhappy household and eventually someone's dismissal. The more Dorothy Fielding thought about her new employee, the happier she was with the thought. After discussing it with Agnes, she went directly to the drawing room and began to write her letter of response to Joan in Ballygwin.

Mary Cecilia's ship, the SS PRESIDENT ROOSEVELT sailed for Boston harbor on March 18, 1923, the day after her eighteenth birthday.

Thomas was angry at his wife for arranging Mary Cecilia's passage and a job with the Fieldlings. For the first time in their married life, Joan had shouted her feelings at him. Thomas, unable to cope with the truth in Joan's angry words, went on a drinking binge. When he was finished with the drinking, he passed out for three days.

As the weeks passed, young Tomasin waited for the postman everyday. He was watching a letter from Mary Cecilia. Everyone in the family missed their darling girl but Tomasin, only nine, did nothing to hide his feelings.

"Mam, why doesn't she write? I miss her."

"Oh Tomasin, be patient, a letter should be coming soon. You know a letter takes at least three weeks, sometimes a month. Here, help me with the garden, the flowers will be blooming soon."

Several days later, the postman called out to Tomasin as he came up the lane.

"Anyone here waitin' on a letter from America?" Tomasin ran to meet the postman before he could move another step.

"Mam, Mam, the letter is here!" Tomasin shouted as he danced towards the cottage with the letter held high.

They were the only two at home. Mam pulled out a chair from the table and settled herself down. Then she reached over and gently pulled Tomasin onto her lap and kissed his cheek.

"Let's read this together" and she adjusted the glasses sitting on the bridge of her nose.

Dear Mam, Da, Mikeen, Paddy and Tomasin,

I arrived safely in Holyoke yesterday. The sea journey was long but I did meet other young travelers that helped to pass the time with me. The meals were good and Mam would be proud of me, using all the forks and spoons correctly. I noticed some of the other passengers waited to see what I would use before they picked up one. Mrs. Fielding is good to me with a warm welcome indeed. She told me to rest today. Tomorrow I can start to learn my job. She is just as you described Mam, but she has grey hair. Her children are grown and away with their own families. She sends you her love.

I can not believe the size of this place. It is so busy. I wonder will I ever get the hang of it.

I miss you all and send you my fondest love.

Your loving daughter,
Mary Cecilia

Thomas cried when he read the letter that night.

"Oh, to think me drinking is the cause of this pain. I chased my little darlin' away and now she is lost to me. Will I ever see her again as long as I live? Sweet Jesus, what have I done?"

Silence was the only response. Joan and the three boys just looked at the floor. Thomas took a deep breath and then started to ramble again.

"As God is my witness, I am givin' up the drink tonight. No more. I won't let it hurt us again."

Joan lifted her head and spoke softly, "Thomas, I hope the Lord will hear your prayer. We are so tired of it all, but we will help, if you let us. We are all hurtin' over the drink. It is an evil force but it can be conquered. Look at Martin from Brandon, sure he has beaten it, but not without a struggle."

The boys remained silent, listening to every word.

Thomas bowed his head and nodded up and down in agreement with Joan. She rose and crossed the room to her husband. She put her hand on his shoulder while she spoke to the boys.

"Time for bed, lads. Tomorrow will be a better day for all of us. Your father is going to try and we have to help him. Now blow out the lamp and sleep soundly."

Ballygwen
Four Years Later

Mikeen surveyed his reflection in the mirror. He was pleased with the image that smiled back at him. He was using Michael for his name now, no longer the childhood Mikeen. He was wearing the new shirt that his father had purchased for him in Tralee just yesterday. It was part of his new suit and shoes for the journey to America, his start at a new life. It was a chance to make something of himself and a chance to send some money home to the family; a little bit of help to get through the hard times.

Michael pushed the thoughts of America out of his mind. Tonight was special in its own way. Tonight was the Carnival Coeli under the big tent and Maureen O'Reilly was sure to be there along with every other teen from twenty miles around.

The carnival came once a year to the village of Cloghane and tonight was the night! Everyone had been talking of the grand night last year, reliving its excitement as the anticipation grew for this year to be even bigger and better.

Michael started to whistle as he finished combing his hair and adjusted his belt. He called out to his brothers.

"Get a move on ye, Paddy, we don't want to be late!"

"Tomasin, remember what I told you, no foolishness with your friends to embarrass us tonight. When you are older, you'll like the girls yourself!"

The three boys scurried around the cottage as Joan smiled at all the anticipation. She and Thomas would go down to the tent a little later and stand with the other folks to enjoy the music, and the laughter. If the music were lively, they would have a dance or two themselves.

There would be no pints tonight. Thomas had been dry for four years.

This achievement had not come easy for Thomas. He struggled to keep sober in an environment that encouraged drinking in its social settings. For the first six months following his resolution not to drink, Thomas remained close to the cottage. His only social outing each week was to church; to chance a stop at the pub was too risky.

Joan tried to help by inviting neighbors to stop in at the cottage more often than usual. She kew, too well, that Thomas was missing the camaraderie of his friends. The neighbors couldn't believe the new Thomas. They had known him for years, but his gradual deterioration had become the norm and the Thomas they saw now was a new man.

There was a young priest assigned to the Cloghane Chapel. His name was Fr. Sean and he knew about Thomas and his struggle. Fr. Sean made the lengthy hike to and from Ballygwen every Wednesday. He coached Thomas, counted another week of progress and tried to keep him motivated. Fr. Sean also met with Thomas after Mass on Sundays. Two years of this routine dragged by, until Thomas had a new pride in himself. He looked better, walked taller and worked harder for himself, Joan, for the boys. The cloud of despair that hung over the little cottage was gone.

As the boys stepped out of the cottage and into the January night, there was a fine mist settling onto Ballygwen. At the crossroads ahead, the boys met several of their friends.

"Michael, when are ye leaving us, lad?" called out his schoolmate, Mike Grainey.

"On the 14th of this month," replied Michael.

"Are ye by any chance going on the U.S.S. ROOSEVELT?"

"Aye."

"I heard that Sean Dillon from Dingle would be on that ship. My father and his are old friends from the Dingle market, but my father just heard the news today. Maybe ye'll get to travel with Sean."

"Sure, I'll be looking for a friendly face, that I will. And if that friendly face is from the Kingdom of Kerry, so much the better!"

"Be sure to stop by our cottage for a spot of tea before you take off, lad. Don't just disappear one day like that Brian Doyle, who never bothered to give a good bye to anyone, and weren't we all planning a nice send-off for him!"

"It'll have to be on Sunday. Uncle Dan is taking me to Castlegregory for the train to Tralee. From there, it's another train to Queenstown. The train only goes to and from Queenstown on a Monday. I can't wait until Thursday, as I'd like."

"Sunday it is."

The sound of an approaching horse and cart stopped the conversation and the boys turned to see Mr. O'Shea approaching. He called out to them in a jolly voice, "Don't ye know the dance is under the tent, lads? What are ye standing at the crossroads for?"

Everyone laughed and fell in step behind the cart, which was loaded with all the O'Shea family, out for an evening of fun. The three Finn brothers split up as they entered the huge tent, each to join with his friends. Michael took a quick scan around the crowd as he entered. No sign of Maureen yet. He thought it might be too early for her to arrive since she was coming from the next village over the strand. That is why he had only met her a few weeks ago at the marketplace. Every Sunday at church, he had watched her from a distance hoping that someday he would muster the courage to speak to her. But it was difficult, with his cousins and parents there. Much too complicated he had decided. Last week, when his Da needed some leather to make shoes, Michael had volunteered to make the trip to the market. There he had met her, standing alone and waiting for a friend.

Michael seized the moment and started a conversation. Yes, she knew about the carnival and yes, she was going and yes, she would see him there. His mind had thought of nothing else for days.

The beat of the music brought his thoughts back to the tent as he and the rest of the crowd parted to make room in the center for the first round of dancers. The crowd was animated and the sounds of happy feet on the wooden flooring made the entire tent seem to dance with the rhythm. The fiddlers kept the pace moving and soon the crowd had sorted itself into groups to dance the sets. Michael joined in with some of the neighbors as they whirled around the floor. He was by far the best dancer of the group and with his dark, curly hair and shining blue eyes, there wasn't a girl who didn't notice him.

The evening was well on its way when Michael saw Maureen arrive with her brother. To Michael's surprise and delight, Maureen smiled directly at him and motioned for him to come over. With his heart pounding, Michael crossed the floor to where she stood.

"Michael, this is my brother Kevin."

"Pleased to meet you, Kevin."

"Aye, Maureen tells me you're going to America. Good luck!"

The music changed to a waltz and Michael asked Maureen to dance. They stepped onto the floor and with a swing they were on their way. It was a wonderful night! The evening ended with the National Anthem and the crowd dispersed slowly wishing the music could go on and on, sad to see such enjoyment end. Michael escorted Maureen outside where they met her brother. Kevin told them neighbors offered them a ride in the pony and cart.

"We'll all meet at the crossroad," directed Kevin and he left to say goodnight to friends. Michael and Maureen started down the lane towards the Crossroads.

"I had a wonderful time tonight," smiled Michael.

"Me too."

"I wish we had met earlier," complained Michael. "It's me own fault. For months I wanted to say hello and I was too shy. To think, now that we know each other, I'm going to be leaving in ten days. Now I wish I weren't going."

"Do you really mean that, Michael? I mean, do you really like me?"

"Aye," said Michael in a whisper.

"Michael, there is something I must tell you."

Michael's mind raced trying to imagine what was coming next. Did she like someone else? Maybe she was only teasing him and she didn't really enjoy the dance. Was he a fool to think that such a young woman would find him attractive? Maureen reached over and took Michael's hand in hers. She saw the concern in his eyes.

"Michael, 'tis good news. I am leaving for New York in three months."

Michael couldn't believe his ears. She was going too! "Where? When?" He couldn't get all his questions out quickly enough. She laughed at his excitement and explained that her cousins lived in New York and they had arranged for her to come in April. They would be together again in the Spring, in a new life, in a new city.

With the sadness lifted, Michael and Maureen continued down the lane towards the Crossroads, hand in hand, oblivious to the rest of the world and animated in plans for the future. They didn't hear the horse and rider approach until they were almost upon them. Michael looked up and called out to the familiar face.

"Good evening, Father McGuire."

"Don't Good Evening me, you brash young man. What do you think you're doing out here alone in the middle of the night with that innocent young thing!" With that he turned his anger to Maureen and screamed at her.

"Don't you know better than to be putting yourself in such a situation and having no self-respect like any decent woman."

That was all Michael could take. It was one thing for Father McGuire to start on him but to attack Maureen for no reason at all. Michael stepped toward the priest in an attempt to explain, when he heard the sound and felt the pain before he actually saw the horsewhip, that hit him repeatedly on the shoulders and around the head. He put his arms up for protection and felt the stings continue on his knuckles. In another instant it stopped as quickly as it had started and the strange man of the cloth rode away on his horse.

Maureen was crying and trying to help Michael to his feet. Michael could not believe the depth of his anger and his humiliation. He vowed he would never forget it.

Michael was preparing to leave and he knew that it was going to be an emotional time for him. Ever since he could remember, whenever he was emotional, his tears would start. He secretly believed that the fairy King of Tears had touched him at birth. He tried to control it, but the tears always won. Embarrassed, he devised a couple of behaviors to help him cope. He would put his hands in his pockets, lower his head and push earth around with his shoe. Most people watched the shoe and missed his face. Another defense was to take out his handkerchief and fake a series of sneezes. He would finish by saying, "What is blowing in the wind today? Makes me sneeze and me eyes water."

But on this day, leaving Ballygwen, there was no defense that would work for Michael. He was crying as he said "Goodbye," and he was not ashamed.

There had been a huge send off party two nights earlier and the tears had started to seep out quietly. He knew that these parties were called an Irish wake, because a son leaving would never be seen again. That night, the impact of his decision to leave Ballygwen hit him hard. What had he been thinking? Surely, his heart must be showing through his shirt, it was beating so wildly and his face burning, as if with fever.

Now the final farewell time had arrived. He felt relief when his Uncle Danny's pony and cart appeared on the lane to take him to Castlegregory and the evening train. Only Father was going to ride along, so this was goodbye to Mam, Paddy and Tomasin. Michael moved quickly, hugged each one, threw his case into the cart and climbed on board. Mam and his younger brothers stood watching until the cart disappeared over the rim of a hill.

When the three men drew near to Castlegregory, Da mentioned to Michael that Aunt Julia and all her family were expecting them to make a stop at Forge Road before going to the train. Aunt Julia was Michael's favorite. His throat began to tighten again and his stomach felt queasy at the thought of more farewells. Unable to tell Da and Uncle Danny how upset he felt, Michael lied about the train schedule, saying there wouldn't be time to stop, they needed to continue directly to the station. Unfamiliar with the schedule, the two men agreed that it was best not to chance missing the train.

Aunt Julia sat by the window all afternoon, watching for Michael. Every half hour or so, one of her own nine children would come running into the kitchen asking if Michael was here yet. She would shoo them out into the yard with a promise to call as soon as he did arrive. As evening approached, she heard the lonesome whistle of the train in the distance and realized Michael was on his way. She moved the chair from the window, returned it to its place at the kitchen table and began to prepare supper. She understood. She knew in her heart that she would never see Michael again. She closed her eyes to remember the smiling face and said a prayer for his safe journey. The leaving was painful.

City and Port of Queenstown, Co. Cork

Queenstown was built into the side of a craggy cliff overlooking Cork Harbor. The water is deep enough for ships to navigate and well protected during storms.

The city is a maze of crooked narrow streets that meander their way between the Cathedral at the summit of the hill to the bustling wharf at the bottom. In between the cathedral and the wharf, there is a collection of assorted houses, shops, eateries, cobblers, and tailors. Every service one might need if leaving or arriving was available here.

As Michael's train approached the city he got his first glimpse of the Cathedral and the bay. When he arrived at the Queenstown station, a young lad named Sean met him. It was Sean's job to show Michael the way to Mrs. Leary's boarding house. The trains brought a steady stream of passengers to the port city every afternoon but the ships loaded and sailed just after dawn each morning, requiring most passengers to stay overnight in Queenstown. Mrs. Leary's name was well known in the Ballygwen area as someone who could be trusted.

Sean and Michael climbed the twisting streets together. Mrs. Leary's place was in the center of everything on Prince Street. When Michael arrived, there were six other passengers already seated for the evening meal. Michael joined the table. He ate heartily and after dinner, everyone lined up for a lice hair check by Mrs. Leary. She was checking because the medical examiners would be checking each passenger in the morning. If Mrs. Leary found lice, she treated the hair that evening with kerosene, shampoo and a special comb. By morning, the scalp and hair would be clear. If the examiners found lice, they would shave your head. On this evening, everyone's head was clear and there was a collective sigh of relief.

"Go on lads and lassies off to bed with you now. Have yerself a good sleep. You'll need to be alert in the mornin'. I will call when its time to rise. You wash and come down. The breakfast will be on the table. After breakfast, Sean will load all the cases onto the cart and meet you at the bottom of the hill by the wharf. You can pay me your two pounds tonight to get it out of the way for the mornin'. Any questions for me now?"

There was silence from the little group.

"Then, God bless you all and have a safe journey."

Michael woke long before the wakeup call. He dressed and left Mrs. O'Leary's quietly by the back door. He climbed the remainder of the hill to the Cathedral. He went inside and looked around at the massive columns and stained glass windows. Having been at home when Mary Cecilia left, he knew how much his parents and brothers would be missing him.

He knelt in the pre-dawn darkness. His prayer was a simple one.

"May their grief be gentle."

PART V

NEW YORK CITY

New York City
February 1927

"**D**AMN THAT DOORBELL," bellowed Mrs. Daedy. She struggled to move her heavy frame out of the overstuffed armchair. She was well known for her lazy approach to everything and today proved to be no different. She waddled across the parlor of her brownstone towards the front door.

Mary Finn smiled as the door opened and she saw the round, familiar face of Bridie looking out at her and Michael.

"And who might this handsome lad be?" asked Bridie Daedy.

"Tis me brother, Michael, just arrived to the States. Have you got a room to rent to him, Bridie?"

"Aye, you have the luck of the Great Saints today. I'm after sending a wee lass off to her family in Boston and that gives me a spot. Let's not be talking in the doorway. Come in, come in, I'll put the kettle on."

"Michael doesn't have a job yet," added Mary as the two guests followed Bridie into the cramped kitchen. "If he has a place to stay, he can start to look for a job with the worry of a bed off his mind."

"Aye, so how do you like what you've seen so far, Michael?"

"'Tis grand. I'm lucky to have Mary. She really has learned her way around this city. I'd be lost without her. It's difficult to believe she's only here four years, she moves around like a native."

The kettle whistled, tea was made, cake passed around and the three Kerry people enjoyed news of home and old friends across the sea. Three hours flew by.

Mary left Michael at Mrs. Daedy's that night. She also left money for the trolley and a newspaper filled with help wanted ads.

After three days of exhausting effort, Michael continued to search for a job but his spirits were taking a beating. Getting used to the crowded streets, the gridlock of traffic and the overall noise and hustle made him homesick for the white stretches of sand and the blue ocean of Ballygwen.

As he returned to Mrs. Daedy's one night, her daughter Kathleen met him in the hallway with a letter from home. His mother wrote often and at the end of a wearisome day it was a treat to sit and read her letters. He saved them all in a shoebox. Sometimes, he would take out the shoebox from under his bed and reread all of the letters until his tired eyes would surrender to sleep.

Tonight his shoebox routine was interrupted when Mrs. Daedy knocked on his door.

"Kathleen is going to a dance tonight with two other friends from Mayo. Want to go along?"

"I'm really tired tonight," pleaded Michael, but Bridie would not accept "no" for his answer.

"I can see you've had a tough day but a little fun may be just what you need. You've been spending too much time alone, boy. Go out and meet some people. It will do you the world of good."

Too tired to argue, Michael simply asked, "What time are they leaving?"

"Eight o'clock," beamed Mrs. Daedy. "I'll tell them to expect you and wear the blue shirt, it looks wonderful with your eyes."

Michael's mind responded with a "go to hell," but he dare not say it. He needed this place to stay. A clean bed for a reasonable price was difficult to find and if going to the dance with Kathleen was part of the price, he's have to pay it for awhile, or at least until a job came through.

One of the Irish men he had met at the football game the week before had given him Jimmy Boyle's name. He said Jimmy might be able to get Michael work on the trolley. The very next day Michael hurried down to the trolley yard. Jimmy was nice enough, but he said he couldn't promise anything, try coming back in five days.

Tomorrow would be the fifth day and the trolley yard was going to be Michael's first stop in the morning. He was growing tired of rejection. He wondered how much of the story old man Sullivan told was actually truth. According to Sullivan, it was easier for the Irish to find work now. Only fifteen years before, offices in New York posted signs in the windows, "No Irish Need Apply." If it was easier to get a job now, it sure didn't seem that way to Michael.

Wednesday morning found Michael up early and off to the trolley yard. He wanted to be the first man to see Jimmy Boyle when he arrived. If there was a job to be had, Michael had no intention of letting someone else beat him to the punch.

Jimmy threw Michael a scowl and cursed under his breath at another worker as Michael entered the small office. Today isn't looking too good, thought Michael. He waited all morning but Jimmy wouldn't see him. Lunchtime came and went but Michael just sat. He could see Jimmy through the window. The man was a whirl of activity; shouting orders and directing men to various locations.

Supper came and went. Michael sat. Somewhere around seven that evening, Jimmy Boyle put on his cap to call it a day and head home. He slammed the office door and started to leave when he spotted Michael, still sitting on the bench.

"I like your attitude, kid. You showed up today like I told ya. You kept your nose in place all day and you're still here. I like a man who doesn't complain. Come back tomorrow, you've got the job."

The phone rang on the second floor of the hospital and the receptionist beckoned Mary over to the telephone.

"Call for you. It sounds like your brother."

"Mary, I've got a job!"

Life was starting to fall into place for Michael. He was comfortable enough at Mrs. Daedy's. Once in awhile, he suffered through an evening with Kathleen to keep the old lady happy and he loved his job and the other men. One detail in his life disturbed him. He had received only one letter from Maureen. It made no sense to him. He had been writing faithfully ever since his ship put into New York. Mary told him not to worry, the mails were slow and letters from home sometimes arrived months after they were written.

Deep inside, somewhere in his gut, or maybe it was a whisper in his ear, something told him it was all over. Maureen wasn't going to write again and he had been a fool to believe she would.

Michael never suspected that Mrs. Daedy was hiding Maureen's letters.

May 1927

This alley was the darkest place Michael had ever been. This is stupid, stupid, stupid. I should run while I still have the chance. There was a quick scampering sound behind him and he knew instinctively it was a rat. He turned to see the two beady eyes glaring at him from under an old newspaper. Mike tightened his grip on the stick. He had come prepared for a little excitement but now the excitement was giving way to terror. He should never have let Mrs. Daedy talk him into this deal.

Now it was too late for turning back. He could see the truck headlights approaching the alley. The headlights were suddenly dimmed and the large vehicle rolled silently to a stop. Two men got out. The big one handed Mike the keys to the cargo area and told him to start unloading and stack the boxes by the wall. Mike did as he was told. He worked silently for at least an hour. Hauling, lifting, stacking. Finally, the inside of the truck was empty and the men turned to leave.

"Tell the old lady we want the money on Thursday. Tell her not to be late." Mission completed, they left the alley as quietly as they came.

Beads of sweat rolled down Michael's face and dampened the collar of his shirt. He wasn't sure if the moisture was from the work or the adrenaline that pumped through his body. He had thought this would be an easy twenty spot, a simple way to pick up the equivalent of two weeks wages. Mary was getting married this month, he could use the extra dollars. He had also heard the stories of people getting rich from prohibition and it sounded so easy. "Like taking candy from a baby," the men would say in the trolley yard. Now he wasn't so sure.

He was beginning to see Mrs. Daedy in a new light. She was a shrewd businesswoman. Every Friday and Saturday night she would host an open party for the young Irish at her place. They would come together in groups, anxious to see a familiar face that would remind them of home and maybe, if they were lucky, take away some of the sting from being thousands of miles away. They would sing and dance and always, there was the hooch.

In the beginning he didn't realize where it came from, he didn't really care. It was just there and available. He drank it like everyone else. He must have been at Daedy's six months before he started to realize that the hefty income in the house was not from the boarders, but from the hooch. The boarders attracted their friends to the house parties like bees to honey. It had all been very carefully planned by Bridie Daedy. She bought the bottle of hooch for twenty-five cents and then sold it by the glass, ten glasses to the bottle at ten cents each. The all night parties were making her a rich woman.

One Sunday morning she approached Michael with a "business deal," as she called it. Cover the alley on 23rd Street for two hours and earn a twenty. Her deliveries needed unloading and protection. So, here he was in the dark.

When Michael got back to the house, the usual Saturday night crowd had begun to assemble. Two of the young men came over to Michael.

"We heard a rumor. Heard that Bridie let you do a delivery. You sure are lucky. We've been begging her for a year, with no luck."

Michael was shocked that others knew, so he didn't answer. He just stood there. The guys interpreted his silence as satisfaction, so they continued babbling.

"If you ever need any help, just give us a shout. We'd be proud to work with you."

The following week when Michael returned to the alley, it didn't seem quite as dark and by the end of six months, the alley held no fear at all.

Ballygwen
August 1927

"Tomasin, run to the well like a good lad, and tell your mother there is a letter here, just arrived, from Mary Cecilia. She'll want to come home."

"Aye, Da." And the thirteen-year-old sprinted down the lane.

Thomas put the kettle on to boil water and set the cups on

the table. When Joan returned, they would read the letter together and have a cup of tea. This letter was overdue and he anticipated that Mary Cecilia had been busy lately. Joan and Tomasin came into the cottage together.

"Where is Paddy gone?" asked Joan.

"He's gone to Seamus O'Flaherty's, returning the shoes I mended."

"Oh, he'll be awhile so, we'll start without him."

The three pulled up chairs to the table, Thomas poured the tea and Joan began reading aloud.

> Dear Mam, Da, Paddy and Tomasin,
>
> I have wonderful news. Bill Broderick has asked me to marry him. His family is from Abbeyfield, Limerick and he has been in New York for six years now. I have given it much thought and believe we can build a good life for ourselves. Bill works in Manhattan. He is doing well. We have been dating over a year now and I do love him.
>
> Although I know you will be sad, not to be at the wedding, I hope you will be excited for me. Michael will be our best man. He and Bill have become friends over the year.
>
> Bill and I are saving what we can and hope to find an apartment convenient to the trolley. How I wish you were here to meet Bill and spend time with us and Michael. Please write and tell me I have your blessings. It will mean the world to me.
>
> Your loving daughter,
> Mary Cecilia

"Ah, I am not surprised. She's been writing about Bill for a year," sighed Joan.

Thomas looked to the roof, as if some words were written there. "'Tis a big step. I hope she'll be happy."

They drank some tea, and then Tomasin spoke. "Mam, please read the letter again."

Joan complied and this time when she finished, Tomasin

asked in a quiet voice, "Does getting married in America mean Mary Cecilia won't be coming home?"

New York City
September 1927

Mary Cecilia Finn and William Broderick were married on a fine Sunday afternoon in New York City. The trees in Central Park were beginning to show the reds and gold of autumn and the late afternoon sun glowed on the skyscrapers. The date was September 11, 1927, eight months after Michael's arrival.

There were about twenty-five guests, an assortment of friends from work, friends from home and friends from the new life. Afterwards, the bride and groom rode in a taxi for the short distance to their new apartment and the waiting celebration.

There were many thoughtful gifts but the most outstanding was a silver tea server set. The shiny teapot sat proudly in the middle of a silver tray surrounded by a gleaming sugar bowl and creamer set. Mary's eyes danced with delight when she opened the huge box.

"How did you ever manage such a beautiful gift, Michael?"

"It is way too much," added Bill, with surprise in his voice.

"I wanted something special for the two of you. Something that says New York. Something for a new beginning and when I saw this, I just knew you would love it."

"Oh, it's beautiful altogether." Mary squeezed Michael in a bear hug and Bill shook Michael's hand while hugging his shoulders with the other arm. The three of them stood around the table admiring the gift.

Later, Mary Cecilia and Michael spoke quietly to each other.

"Mam would love to see you so happy and so beautiful," said Michael.

"Aye, it is the only thing missing this day."

"Ah, the distance is a terrible curse. 'Twould be wonderful to have them here or for us to be there."

Wedding Day
New York, 1927
Mary Cecilia Finn and William Broderick
Michael Finn, Best Man, on the right.

Spring 1928

"Hey Mike, look at this notice. We're moving up to the big time now. Says here the trolley line is merging with the city subway line."

Michael extended his hand, "Let me read that."

His friend, Riley, was whirling in a circle with outstretched arms. "Today is our lucky day! Man, we just died and went to heaven!"

Michael watched Riley and shrugged his shoulders. "It's only a merger. So what."

"So what? Mike, my good man, don't you understand. We work for the City now. We'll get paid for Christmas and you won't lose your job the first day you're out sick. I'm telling ya man, this is our lucky day. Let's get a beer after work and celebrate."

Two weeks later, there was a second notice posted.

In accordance with merger regulations,
All employees are to present birth certificates or other
proof of age to the office clerk, no later than Friday.

How will I handle this? Michael had the paperwork, but he wasn't about to share it with the clerk. The problem was not his paperwork, it was his birthday. The minimum age for trolley work, and now the city subway, was twenty-one. Michael had always looked older than his age and when he was first hired no one asked about his age. He had enjoyed two months of paychecks before a clerk asked for his proof of age and Michael discovered for the first time, there was a minimum age requirement. He had successfully stalled with a series of excuses.

"I have my papers at my sister's home. I'll get them on my day off."

"My sister is away in the country, she'll be back next month. I can get it then."

"I worked my regular day off, couldn't get to my sister's this week."

He would try stalling again. He only needed to buy three

months, since he would be twenty-one in July. It was now the end
of July and he carried his birth certificate in his back pocket. He
was waiting for the clerk to ask again and then he would produce
the valuable document.

This time, the clerk put a note on his paycheck. He went
immediately to the office and handed over his birth certificate.

"Mike, I must be dreaming. Is this finally your birth certificate?"

Michael laughed and tried to sound sincere. "Sorry for the
delay." He was nervous and shifted his weight from foot to foot.
He could feel the beads of sweat rolling down his back and soaking
his shirt. What would come next? Would the clerk pay enough
attention to the date and realize why he had stalled? Would he
fire him on the spot for working prior to his birthday? Michael
held his breath.

"I see I missed your birthday. Just passed a few weeks ago."

Michael's dry mouth prevented him from answering so he
nodded his head.

The clerk folded the document carefully and handed it back
to Michael with a smile and a wink. "I hope it was a good one."

Michael was afraid to move from his spot. He returned the
certificate to his back pocket and waited.

"That's all I needed, Mike. Your file is complete now."

"Thank you," came from Michael's lips. He turned slowly and
expecting any moment to hear, "wait" or "come back" he headed
slowly for the exit door. He placed his hand tentatively on the
door knob. Still no sound from behind him. He turned the knob,
heard it click to an open position, pulled the door open and
walked out of the office. Once on the other side, with the door
closed tightly behind him, he let out a whoop of delight and ran
the entire length of the hallway to the men's room.

New York was bustling these days. The economy was strong
and jobs were plentiful. The general mood of the city was upbeat.
Michael was busy looking for a new place to live. His patience had
run out with Mrs. Daedy and her less than intelligent daughter,
Kathleen. Once he had the money saved for his sister's wedding

gift, he had stopped the alley work and Bridie Daedy was none too pleased. That, combined with his obvious dislike for Kathleen, created uncomfortable feelings in the house. Besides, he was learning his way around the city and had outgrown his need for the safety of the boarding house. He was ready for his own place. He spent every spare moment reading the newspaper ads and on his days off, visiting these places.

Michael needed a place to call his own, a place with some privacy that still fit into his budget. He was sending money home to Ballygwen each month and trying to save a few dollars for himself, for the future. He wasn't sure what his future would be just yet. He thought about it often. Right now, he had three goals on his mind, help the folks, find a new place to live and open a savings account. His payday was Thursday, and this week, his day off was Friday. He planned to open a savings account at the Bank of the United States, even though he would have to pass three other banks along the way. He liked the sound of it. The Bank of the United States. He was in the United States now and he wanted to be a part of it. The Bank of the United States would be his bank.

New York City, USA
Arrival Day, May 1929

There was a buzz in the air as Mollie's ship glided past the towering Statue of Liberty. Everyone on board was excited to arrive in New York and anxious to get back on dry land. Suitcases, string tied parcels and bags of every description were beginning to appear on the deck in anticipation of leaving the ship. Mollie and Maureen were standing by the rail as the tug met the huge ship and nuzzled it into its berth on the West Side of New York City.

The ship held seventeen hundred passengers so disembarking was a long process. The girls were beginning to get impatient after the months of preparation at home followed by the long voyage. Three hours later, their names were called and they walked down the gangway to a new life.

They had a seat on the designated waiting bench. Within minutes, Mollie could see Uncle Pat approaching the desk. The immigration official signaled the girls to join them.

"Sir, what is your relationship to Mary Lynch?"

There was a delay and when Uncle Pat was slow to respond, Mollie jumped in with a response. "He is my uncle." The clerk looked over his spectacles but ignored Mollie.

"Sir, what is the address where Miss Lynch will be residing?"

Again, there was a delay in Uncle Pat's response, Mollie volunteered, "139 West 101st Street."

"One more word out of you Miss and you will be back on that ship, going back where you came from," said the agitated clerk. Mollie bit her lower lip.

Once the paperwork was completed, Uncle Pat introduced the woman that was standing with him. She was Mary Galligan from Cavan, and her brother-in-law, Jimmy Galligan, was Mollie's godfather. Uncle Pat rented a room from her and her husband, Matty. The Galligan household was now the destination for the girls.

"Call me Aunt Mary," said Mrs. Galligan. "Welcome to New York. We've been expecting you. You girls must be famished. Let's go home, have some tea and put on the dinner."

They were a strange looking group of four as they walked the long city blocks to the subway. Aunt Mary led the way while the girls struggled to keep pace, dragging their suitcases. Uncle Pat walked to the rear of the group, as if he didn't belong with them. His mind was preoccupied. Thank goodness for Mary Galligan. What would he ever do with these two females, if she weren't there to help him? He was feeling overwhelmed and began to wonder why it had seemed like such a good idea when he had invited them to New York. Today, it seemed like an insurmountable struggle awaiting them all.

They descended the flight of steps leading to the subway station and Uncle Pat finally jumped to the front of the group, giving each woman the needed coin for the fare. Five cents for each. The girls were awed by everything around them. The size of the station, the crowds of people, the swiftness of the subway cars, and the variety of skin colors. There were two men dark as coal and a woman the color of coffee. There was a Chinese woman holding her small son's hand. Before today, Mollie had only seen a picture of Chinese people in a schoolbook.

The girls weren't sure about subway routines so they carefully watched Aunt Mary and Uncle Pat then imitated their behavior. They sat side by side with the cases sandwiched between them. At one point, Mollie glanced over at Maureen and chuckled when she saw Maureen's mouth gaping at the high fashion of the passengers. Mollie stopped her chuckle abruptly when it occurred to her that her country dress probably looked as out of place as Maureen.

Aunt Mary motioned to them that they were getting off the train. Mollie tightened her grip on the suitcase, took a deep breath and stood tall as the wheels of the subway car came to a screeching stop. They exited the subway at 96th Street and Broadway, on the West Side of Manhattan. It was a short walk to the brownstone building the Galligans called home.

The Galligans lived on the top floor of a four-story building. Their rooms were large and the windows in the living room faced the street. These eight-foot high windows were the tallest Mollie had ever seen in anyone's home. She was impressed with the lace curtains that graced the glass panes.

The entrance into the apartment was through a door located in the dining room. There was a large table and six chairs in the center of the room and to the rear of the dining room, there was a small but functional kitchen.

Mary Galligan entered her home with enthusiasm and a light step. She had an efficiency of motion. With one hand she was removing and hanging her hat while the other retrieved her large apron from a wall hook. She called over her shoulder to the girls.

"Just put your cases in the corner for now. Pat will show you the bathroom; I put towels in there for you to wash up. We will eat in just awhile."

Mollie examined every detail of the bathroom. It was going

to be a luxury to have indoor plumbing. When she was in Clareboy she had heard so much about the beautiful bathtubs, showers and toilets of New York. In the cottage, you used a chamber pot during the night or when it rained. Otherwise you went outside behind a barn or the shed. Now, she marveled silently at the softness of the toilet tissue and contented herself with washing her hands and face. A bath with running water and the privacy of a separate room was a treat for later.

Mollie Lynch
New York City, 1929

When she returned to the living room, Uncle Pat appeared to be more confident in his familiar surroundings. He spoke to her like the Uncle Pat she remembered from his visit to Cavan. Aunt Mary had the dinner ready in a flash and the girls set the table. It was the best meal since they left home. The journey was truly over; this was their new home. They were finishing the dishes when the door opened with the chatter of children spilling into the room. Aunt Mary's two children, Matty Junior and Rosemary were home from school. They were polite to the new visitors but in ten minutes they were out the door to play with friends.

The apartment had four bedrooms: one for each child, one for Mary and Matty with the last for their boarder, Uncle Pat.

It was decided that Mollie would sleep on the couch and Maureen on a folding cot that was stored in the closet during the day. The girls stood their cases in a corner of the dining room, out of Mary's way and did their best to be model houseguests.

Mary's husband, Matty, arrived home in the early evening. A warm-hearted man, he gave the girls a hug, welcomed them to his home and then settled into his favorite armchair for the evening. As the girls soon learned, if Matty was home, he was in his chair. Next to the chair was a small table with Matty's pipe rack and a can of Prince Albert Tobacco.

The "Greenhorns," as the newly arrived Irish were called, settled in over the next few days. Aunt Mary introduced them to a friend named Rose McConnell, a woman in her mid-forties. Rose had been in New York for many years and was employed in a physician's household on Fifth Avenue. When Rose first heard about Patrick's plans to sponsor Mollie and also bring Maureen to New York, she volunteered to assist with all the plans. Rose was excited for weeks about the girls arrival. Today,

Rose arranged to take the girls shopping and within a few hours, both Mollie and Maureen were outfitted in the latest fashion.

When they returned to the Galligan household, the four women had a chat about plans for the future. Always full of energy and enthusiasm, Rose announced that she would be back tomorrow to take Mollie to a nearby hospital that posted vacancies. Maureen, on the other hand, needed to report to a school. Maureen was only sixteen and seven months of age. Since she did not have a relative sponsoring her, she needed to attend school until her seventeenth birthday. Mollie was still fifteen, over a year younger, but since her uncle was sponsoring her, she was allowed to chose between school or employment and Mollie wanted to work. On Tuesday morning, Aunt Mary walked to the nearest school with Maureen while Mollie and Rose went to the hospital.

Mollie couldn't wait to tell Aunt Mary the good news. She rushed up the stairway ahead of Rose.

"I got the job! I got the job!" she shouted to other tenants she met in the hall and to anyone else who would listen.

Mary and Maureen heard the commotion on the stairway and met Mollie just inside the dining room door.

"Great news. Tell us, tell us."

"I start on the first of June. And would you believe, thirty dollars a month! I'm so happy I could pinch myself."

By now Rose had climbed the stairs, entered the room and joined the group.

"I get to share a room with one other person and all my meals and uniforms are included. And we saw the rooms, they are large and I have my own closet and share the bathroom."

Rose stood smiling behind Mollie and decided not to interrupt the enthusiastic outburst.

Aunt Mary spoke next. "What will you be doing at the hospital?"

"I am going to work in the nurses dining room. Can you imagine? They have a dining room just for the nurses! Oh, I just had a thought. What time did they say I should be there on the first day?"

Rose saw the need to get involved, "Never mind that for now. You will be receiving a letter in the next week with all the details.

Aunt Mary spoke next. "Now, Maureen can tell you her good news."

"Yes, we went to the school this morning and since I will be seventeen by September, I only have to attend classes for the month of June and then I can get a job."

Rose responded with outstretched arms, "Good news all around! Let's have tea and cake."

She opened a large shopping bag that she left at Aunt Mary's earlier in the morning when she first arrived. She reached into the bag and lifted out a chocolate bakery cake with Congratulations written across the top in pink letters.

"You had this cake bought already?" said Mollie in disbelief. "How could you have known I would get the position?"

"I didn't," smiled Rose. "I just had confidence in you. Let's celebrate!"

One week later, Mollie was alone in the Galligan house for the first time since she arrived. Matty, Mary, and Uncle Pat were at work. The children and Maureen had left for school. Mollie had one more week before the start of her employment. She decided to pack up her homemade dresses and send them home to mother for her younger sisters. She would be wearing a uniform at the hospital everyday and she had two new dresses purchased with Rose for Church and her days off. As she ironed the dresses, a flood of tears began to flow down her cheeks. She looked at the tiny, neat stitches sewn with so much love. She pictured her mother in the cottage, delighted with the dresses, spending hours to have them fit Mollie perfectly. The feelings of loneliness overwhelmed Mollie. She missed her mother, her father and all the cottage commotion of her brothers and sisters. She stopped her work and sat in Uncle Matty's armchair. Alone for the first time, she cried with loud, shaking sobs. She cried for the days of sickness on the boat, she cried for being fifteen and alone, she cried for one more hug from her mother and one more cup of tea at the fireside. Whatever made me want to leave? If I had known the pain, what choices would I have made?

The next several months were a whirlwind of new experiences. Rose took Mollie to Coney Island on her day off from the hospital. Never had she enjoyed such an outing; the ocean, the rides, the crowds, and her first hot dog!

She rode the subway with Uncle Pat and was left behind when, without warning, he suddenly awoke from his catnap, realized it was his stop, and jumped off. She rode to the next station, exited to the streets above and started to walk. She asked several pedestrians on the street where she could find 139 West 101st Street. They pointed her in the right direction.

Meanwhile, Mary Galligan was aghast when Patrick came home alone.

"Where is Mollie?" she asked.

"Oh, B' Jesus! I forgot all about her. I left her on the train!" said Uncle Pat as he walked to his room and went to bed for the night.

Beside herself with fear for Mollie, Mary Galligan started walking towards the subway station. She and Mollie met about five blocks from the Galligan house and arrived home around two in the morning where they burst into laughter.

Maureen finished school at the end of June and applied for a position at the hospital, using Mollie for a reference. Maureen was hired but her job and dormitory were in a different wing, which meant they seldom saw each other, had different working hours and days off. The girls started to drift apart.

One afternoon, Mollie received a note from Maureen to meet her in the hospital lobby after work. It was important. When Mollie arrived in the lobby, Maureen was crying.

"I have to leave, Mollie."

"What do you mean, leave?"

"I have to leave the hospital. I can't stay here."

"Why? What is going on? Where are you going?"

"I'm pregnant, Mollie. The rules won't allow me to stay here. My boyfriend says I can stay with him for now."

"Now? Are you getting married?"

"He said he'll take care of me. I can't stay here. I've no where else to go."

"Go to Aunt Mary. She'll help."

"No, Mollie. Listen to me. Don't tell. I will write to her and give her an excuse for why I had to leave the hospital. Don't tell her about the baby. I'm too upset."

Clareboy
August 1929

Bridget was concerned about a lengthy hospital stay. She thought of Johnny, her seven children and the cottage. She begged the doctor to let her stay in Cavan Hospital, closer to home.

"You need to see the specialist in Dublin. He knows so much more. For the sake of your husband and children, please go to see him. If anyone can help you, it is this specialist."

Bridget thought about his words and agreed to take the train to Dublin. Bridget's good friend and neighbor, Nora, agreed to stay with the children. Bridget and Johnny left home in mid August. The train ride was tedious for Bridget who was experiencing pains in her back and between her shoulder blades. Johnny was attentive and tried to make the trip enjoyable for Bridget pointing out interesting sites along the way and getting her tea and scones in the dining car.

Johnny had a football friend, Seamus, living about a mile from the center of Dublin. They went to his home from the train and stayed the night. The next day they arrived for Bridget's early morning appointment at Dublin Hospital. The results were what they expected. Surgery was needed, and the sooner the better. After much deliberation, Bridget and Johnny agreed to the surgery. Bridget's left breast was removed.

"I have some bad news for you, Johnny. Your wife will recover from this surgery, but her cancer is too advanced. Take her home and keep her comfortable. It is just a matter of time."

New York City
September 1929

September brought Mollie's sixteenth birthday. The Galligan's and Uncle Pat arranged a Saturday night get together for her with a huge birthday cake. Mollie was thrilled with all the thoughtful cards and gifts.

Rose was helping Aunt Mary in the kitchen.

"Any news of her mother?" whispered Rose.

"We are watching for a letter everyday. The last news was that she went to Dublin to see the surgeon. My knees are bruised from all my praying. It is so hard on Mollie. Sure, she's only a young thing. Imagine only sixteen today, miles away from home and hearing her mother is ill."

Later that night, Mollie hugged Aunt Mary.

"It was a wonderful night. Thank you both for the lovely party. It was so special."

"Not a 'tall. You are a special one to us."

"I'm worried about Mam. It is not like her to miss my birthday. I wonder how the hospital stay is going?"

"Listen to me, child. No news is good news. We must keep praying for good results. Want to go to mass together tomorrow morning? I will phone work and go in late."

"That would be good but, I don't want problems for you at work."

"Not a 'tall, I've been there so long, I'm a fixture."

Six weeks passed before a letter arrived from Mam.

Clareboy
October 20, 1929

Well, my Dear Mollie,

*I suppose you think you will never hear from me again.
Well, thank God, I am able to write again to you. Well Mollie,
I certainly did go through a good deal since but thank God for his
goodness to me, I never suffered one minutes pain in all. I just came
home from Dublin last night. I was away from the 22nd of August
'til last night. I was going the next day after I wrote to you last but
I did not like to tell you. Well dear Mollie, it took me all my time
since I came back to look at everything you sent. God help you, they
got all the clothing you sent and the beads and prayer books, they
are lovely. Well, dear Mollie, I would not know you in the photos,
you gained weight. God spare you your health. As bad as I was
Mollie, I never forgot to pray for you. Well dear Mollie, one thing
annoyed me was that, I was not to be had to send you something
for your birthday, for it was my whole intention but you know
yourself the rest had enough to contend with. Bridgie made great
work. I had just 32 chickens hatched out when I was going away.
They only lost one of them. I thought they would not have half of
them. Well, dear Mollie, I am not writing much now, I will write
a longer letter after awhile. So I will say good bye, hoping to hear
from you soon.*

Your loving Mother

New York City
October 1929

"Oh, no."

"Just hurry, Michael. I'm going home to get my passbook and heading to the bank."

Michael couldn't believe what he was hearing. The stock market had crashed. He was operating his train most of the morning and hadn't heard any radio reports. When he pulled his last run into the train yard, his buddy John was grabbing his coat and running out of the motormen's shack. He stopped long enough to tell Michael the basic facts. There was a run on the banks. Everyone wanted their money and lines were forming for withdrawals at all the banks around the city. Michael froze in his spot. He was trying to digest all the information when two more friends ran past him.

"Don't stand there. Get to the bank."

Michael ran into the shack, grabbed his lunch pail and jacket and tried to catch up with the two men who had just passed him on the pavement. His mind and his legs were moving quickly now. How can this be? I'm sure I am safe. My money is in the Bank of the United States, for God's sake. How much better can you get than that?

Once out of the train yard, he exited onto the street. He wasn't prepared for what was taking place. People were running in different directions. The traffic was snarled. Some people, frustrated with the traffic jam, jumped out and abandoned their cars, hoping to make more progress on foot. Michael felt his heart start to pound inside his chest.

By the time Michael got to The Bank of the United States, its doors were locked tight. There was an angry mob shouting and yelling in front of the building. There were several policemen on horseback but the mere numbers of people kept them from being effective in managing the mob. Some men and women were crying; others were screaming obscenities. Michael couldn't get any reliable information from anyone. It was obvious what had occurred. The market had crashed, people had stormed the banks for their money and the banks unable to comply with the demand, had simply locked the doors.

Would they reopen tomorrow? Was there any money to be distributed, if they reopened? Should he try to stay here overnight and be one of the first on the line in the morning? Were his savings lost, as people were saying? So many questions and no answers.

The crowd was turning violent. People had torn apart a fence from a neighboring property and were now using the pieces of wood like clubs. They were attempting to break into the building but when that was unsuccessful, they turned on each other. The violence increased with shoving and pushing. There were screams from some of the women who were getting trampled. Michael realized this was not the place to be tonight.

Frustrated, angry and upset he started for home. He wanted to call his sister, Mary Cecilia and her husband, Bill. Maybe they had more news than he had gathered. But it was too late, she would have left work by now and neither he nor she had a phone at home. He decided to walk the twenty streets to the Emerald Isle Pub. He had some friends there and the Pub would have the latest radio reports.

He had to squeeze his body into the bar. No one in New York was at home. Everyone was on the streets or in the pubs. His worst fears were confirmed. The banks would not reopen. All his savings were gone. Two years of sweat, toil and deprivation to save his nest egg of five hundred dollars. All gone. He pulled out a fifty-cent piece from his pocket, plunked it on the bar and said, "Whiskey."

Clareboy Cottage

Johnny doesn't remember how he managed the trip home from Dublin. Bridget needed to stay after her surgery, so Johnny went back to the cottage alone. The older children sensed the severity of the situation. Johnny sat down with Patrick, his oldest and Bridgie, now his oldest daughter, at home.

"Mam is sick. The surgeon says she will need lots of care when she comes home. I'm counting on you to help me take care of her. I know it is asking a lot, but we need to be together on this."

"We will help, Da," answered Bridgie. Patrick nodded in agreement.

Nothing more was said. The three of them sat frozen in their seats, staring into the fire.

At the end of two months, Johnny made his final trip to Dublin to bring Bridget home. He struggled to be strong for her. They went home together, as if Bridget had been cured.

New York City
December 1929

The City was struggling to regain its composure. The financial capital of the country was on its knees. There were job layoffs and money was scarce. The infrastructure of the economy was crippled. Many financiers committed suicide rather than deal with their ruination. Houses were lost and food was scarce.

Those who were lucky enough to have employment dug in for the long haul. The situation spread, it was no longer New York alone, the depression set in across the country.

In spite of the depression, in anticipation of Christmas, the city decorated itself in bursts of red and green. Music was everywhere and it was free. The craziness of the time made the words of the Christmas carols more significant. While the native New Yorkers knew Christmas was scaled down, it was a fantasyland for Mollie. As she prepared for her first New York Christmas, the joy of the season was tempered with concern for her mother. Finally, on December 23rd a letter arrived in the mail.

Clareboy

12 December, 1929

My Dear Mollie,

I suppose you are despairing of me answering your kind and welcome letter, which I was glad to get and to see by it that you are well, Thank God. Well, Mollie I am not writing much this time for I am in a poor way with a boil on my back,

it is getting better, Thank God. I did not think I would get
writing at all. I was going to let your father's letter do for us
two. Well, Mollie, I think I will finish for I am tired. I did
not think I would write so much. Good bye, wishing you a
Happy Christmas, I remain your loving mother, to Mollie,
Good bye. XXXXXXXXXX

Clareboy
First Week of January 1930

Gone. Bridget was gone. Buried in the graveyard of Drumkilly Chapel where she was baptized and married. It was a grand funeral, as most would say. Lots of family and neighbors in attendance. The priest gave a moving homily and the seven children alongside Johnny filled the front pew.

It was late evening now and the cottage was quiet. The neighbors had returned home and Johnny was alone with his thoughts and his children. He contemplated how he could only recall snippets of the day. He had tried to concentrate, to store every little detail away for the future, for the younger children when they grow older and for his own comfort. But, as the day progressed, his mind drifted to memories of better times, making it difficult to focus.

His daughter Bridgie would be fifteen in two months, and had taken on the role of mother, once her mother was bedridden. He marveled at her generous spirit. She was everywhere, helping everyone. She anticipated the needs of the little ones, cooked the meals, maintained the family routines and readied the younger children for school in the morning. The boys assumed their mother's garden chores, helped with the forge, fed the small collection of farm animals and hauled water from the well.

Tonight, Bridgie tucked Barney, Dodie and Maggie into bed and helped them with their prayers. He had followed her and kissed them goodnight with assurances that Mam was watching them from heaven. The older boys, John, Larry and Patrick were quietly sitting at the table, not doing much of anything.

"Boys, are the animals taken care of for the night?"

"Aye, Da. We filled the water buckets and readied the kettle on the hearth for the morning porridge," answered John.

"You are good sons. Go to bed, when you are ready. I will look in on you in a bit. I am going out to check the forge."

Outside, in the stillness of the night and the empty forge, he was alone with his thoughts. They were jumbled in his head this past week. Seven children; seven to raise. I must be careful not to make a washerwoman of Bridgie. It is so easy to let her do everything. And little Barney, he is the one too young to remember his loving mother. I must keep her memory alive for him. Young Patrick, sure he's a man himself these days, eighteen next month, but I can tell, the smithy blood does not run in those veins. He will need my help in sorting out his future. But young John, I think he will be the blacksmith. And of course, the little goslings, Larry, Maggie and Dodie. I must see to their schooling.

He sat quietly letting the physical exhaustion settle in, bringing with it some comfort. Ah, if only I could go back in time. I'd ask me own Da how he survived when he lost Rose. I didn't pay enough attention to his stories. I was too busy to listen and now the answers are silent. It's only now I recognize the strength I took for granted. How did he do it?

I wish me brother, Patrick, was here. He was always the thinker between us. Just to sit with him would be a great comfort. He would understand, without me even telling 'em. Ah, it is too much to think about tonight. He returned to the cottage and his empty bed.

Johnny and Barney Lynch

New York City
February 1930

It was two days before the first of February when Mollie received a message from Maureen. Mollie remembered the date because she was looking forward to her paycheck on the first of the month. Mollie sent a Christmas card to Maureen but did not receive one in return. She dismissed it as not important; Maureen had lots to deal with these days. She hadn't seen Maureen since that night in the hospital lobby. The message asked Mollie to meet Maureen at the Coffee Shop on Broadway around eight in the evening.

It was cold as Mollie walked along Broadway. I hope all is well with Maureen, she mused. Maybe she wants to tell me she is getting married or maybe she wants me to be a bride's maid. Wouldn't that be lovely? Perhaps Maureen won't be alone and she will introduce me to her boyfriend. Mollie stopped at the corner and waited for the traffic light to turn green. Only two short blocks to walk and the suspense will be over.

Mollie entered the coffee shop and spotted Maureen sitting alone in a booth. Maureen's pregnancy was just beginning to show and her face had that mother-to-be glow. Maureen waved to Mollie. They ordered one slice of apple pie with ice cream to share, along with a pot of tea. Mollie sensed that Maureen was nervous so she tried not to rush the conversation although she was anxious to hear what was important enough for Maureen to arrange the meeting.

After some small talk and finishing the pie, Maureen cleared her throat and became very serious.

"I wanted you to meet me tonight because I have some important news."

Mollie smiled back at Maureen. Maureen kept a very solemn face.

"It is not good news, Mollie. It is really difficult for me to speak about it, but I am worried that you have not heard yet. Your mother died on the third of January. She was buried at Drumkilly Chapel. My family wrote immediately to get the word to us although they leave me with the heavy burden of telling you. My mother thought it would be awhile before your grieving father would put pen to paper. I am so sorry, Mollie."

Mollie tried to digest the words that were spoken to her. Tears started down her face.

"I knew she was very ill, but I never thought she would die. I just thought I would always have my mother." They sat for a long time and ordered another pot of tea.

"Now I will have to tell Uncle Pat and the Galligans. This will be a long night."

Maureen walked Mollie to the Galligan's house. She stopped when they reached the front steps.

"I won't be going in, Mollie. I haven't told the folks at home about the baby. Can you understand?"

"Yes."

"Again, I'm sorry for your loss. Keep in touch." Then Maureen turned and walked away.

It was March before a letter arrived from Mam's best friend.

Clareboy
17 March, 1930
Dear Mollie,

Just a few lines in answer to your kind letter received some time ago. We were watching to hear from you. I often thought how you could be able to bear the sad news of poor mother's death. I may tell you Mollie, it went very hard on myself, as I always trusted her as my best friend.

Well, dear, when I wrote you last, she was all right, only a boil on her back. No one thought anything of that. We made her go to the doctor. Andy drove herself and your father to Kirwin. He told her take light food and prescribed a few things. When she came out from him your father went in and he told him she was done, that it was only a matter of a short time. I couldn't believe your father when he told me. She went home walking from here, went to bed and never did arise. She told me she was going to die. I laughed and said, you are far from it. And she said, I was dreaming and I seen it all. And if it's the will of God, I don't care. So dear Mollie, she died the happiest death could be. She suffered no pain and never murmured, only about your father. "The poor fellow is killed and run off his feet getting things for me." Everyday she would tell me that. May she rest in peace and God grant we both may be as well prepared to die as your mother was. Everything that could be done was done in time, the priest and doctor and all care. You should be happy to be away and there is enough at home. Poor Bridgie is making great work keeping them clean and everyday at school. Barney and Doddie were here a few minutes ago and he is looking well and a great sport. Little he knows, poor child, the loss of his good mother. Now Mollie, like a good girl, don't forget to have an odd mass for mother, for surely, she thought more about you, so far away, and also be as good as you can to Bridgie. Just imagine if you were in her place, getting all their wants.

Hoping this finds you well and with every good wish. I remain as ever,

Your fond friend,
Katherine

Bridgie and her brother, Barney Lynch

New York City
Spring 1933

Mollie outgrew her position at the hospital. She learned her way around the city, made friends and found a new job paying fifty-five dollars a month as a nanny. She went to live with the Hyman family on East 62nd Street and Park Avenue. Mr. Hyman was an attorney and his wife, a schoolteacher. They had one daughter, Eileen, nine months old when Mollie came to their household. Eileen had big blue eyes and light sandy colored hair. Everyone agreed and laughed that Eileen looked more like Mollie than the Hymans.

Each day Mollie would walk Eileen across Fifth Avenue and into the Central Park playground. On nice days, it was a gathering place for all the nannies in the area.

It was here that Mollie met Lena, another nanny. They liked each other immediately, became friends and met in the park everyday with their young charges. Lena loved to dance and often told Mollie stories of the Galway Hall. It was a dance hall where groups of young Irish would gather on the weekends for Irish music and entertainment. Lena insisted that Mollie come with her, even if she had to switch her night off for one week.

Finally, one Saturday night in September, Mollie met Lena at the Galway Hall. Mollie was amazed at the size of the crowd. She and Lena met some friends and danced several times. The hall was warm and they were overheated from the dancing. Taking a break, they ordered cold drinks. Unable to find seats, they stood against the wall.

"I am so glad that you encouraged me to come."

"And I am so pleased that you finally agreed to meet me."

As they continued to talk, they failed to notice a young man approaching them from the left. He was standing right next to them before they became aware of his presence. He smiled and they smiled back at him. He spoke to Mollie.

"Do you have the time? I am to meet a friend here at 10:30."

Mollie glanced at her wristwatch, "Yes, it's 10:15."

"Thank you. My name is Michael. What's yours?"

Ballygwen
1934

Paddy and Tomasin both had steady girls. Paddy's girl was from Teer and Tomasin's was from Goulane.

Joan and Thomas were happy that both young men appeared to be getting ready to settle down. By all appearances, they would settle nearby and the idea of grandchildren close to their village warmed Joan's heart. Mary Cecilia had two children in America but that was too many miles away to offer comfort.

Although separated by five years, the brothers were close. As Paddy grew, his musical ability was recognized. He was recruited for the marching band of the Irish Free State Army and assigned to the Tralee headquarters. Paddy was home for a visit one weekend when a storm hit the coastline. It appeared, at first, to be a squall approaching and nothing unusual for the area. Instead, the wind shifted direction and increased in velocity. It happened quickly. The men of the Brandon fishing fleet were only one mile from shore and recognized the danger approaching. They tried to outrun the storm, rowing as powerfully as possible. But the clouds opened up with lightening, thunder and pounding rain. The wind churned the small waves into walls of water nearly fifteen feet high. The men continued to row, desperate to reach the pier, or the shoreline. They were fighting for their lives. The curraghs were fast. By design, they cut through waves, maintained balance and handled easily with a skilled and seasoned crew.

Families and friends ran to the shoreline with lanterns. They stood shoulder to shoulder holding the lanterns tight against the whipping wind. They hoped the light would guide the men back to shore. The noise of the storm made it impossible for anyone to speak but words weren't needed. Everyone carried fear of the sea in a corner of his heart. Even on a sunshiny day, they knew the danger of a storm for the fishing fleet.

The men rowing spotted the lights. They were only a half-mile out now. The light gave them energy and renewed their strength to row. The sea was pounding them but they kept rowing, aiming for the lights, the only thing visible in the blinding rain.

But the squall was not about to let the men win the struggle. In an instant the wind changed direction and the wave came from behind, a wall of water now twenty feet high. It broke the curraghs and sent the men tumbling into their graves.

When the storm subsided, the entire Brandon fishing fleet was lost.

Everyone in the village lost someone. For Joan, it was the Fitzgerald cousins. It brought back all the memories of her father, the fisherman Mikeen, and her early years spent on the mountain in Lis. When the sun came up the next morning, she walked to Cloghane, climbed the hill to the cemetery, and left flowers for Mikeen, Mary, Jane and baby Owen.

Clareboy

Maggie was scared. Her knee was feeling worse each day. She hid it for a week, trying not to worry Da. She knew the story of John's arm.

John tripped and fell while working in the vegetable garden. He landed on a pitchfork that had been standing upright in the earth but toppled from John's weight. The timing was exact and to hear Da tell it, "It couldn't happen again in a thousand years." One of the tongs stabbed through John's arm between the elbow and the wrist.

While Patrick and Da washed the wound and applied a tourniquet, Da called out, "Larry fetch the donkey from the back field. We need to take John to the doctor."

Maggie and Rose pulled the cart from its storage spot next to the shed. Barney watched. As they climbed into the cart, Da told the six children remaining at home to mind Patrick and Bridgie while he was away.

When father and son arrived at the country surgery, the doctor examined John's wound and told Da the fee was one pound. "That's fine. Take care of the boy."

"No, that's one pound, payable now."

"Sure I don't have a pound in me pocket. We left in a hurry. I can give you a half pound coin and return tomorrow with the remainder."

"No, that's one pound, payable now."

"But you have my word, I will pay you."

"Sorry, sir, but the fee is one pound, payable now."

"Surely, you know me and my family. Ask any man around, he will tell you Johnny the Blacksmith always pays his debts."

"I'm sorry, sir."

Angry now, Da grabbed the half-pound coin from the table, slapped his cap onto his head and said, "Come John. We'll not be doing business with the likes of this one. I'll be sure to let the neighbors know what happened here today." Outside John spoke, "I'll be fine, Da. Let's go home."

"No, we'll continue to Cavan Town. We will see the pharmacist.

It was now late in the day and the pharmacist was preparing to lock his shop. Da called out to him, "Seamus, please wait. We need your help."

The pharmacist recognized Johnny from the numerous purchases made when Bridget was ill. "Hello, Johnny. What's the problem?" Seamus was appalled at Johnny's story. He used a disinfectant on the boy's arm, closed the wound with two stitches and applied a sterile bandage. "Keep it clean and apply this salve every night. If it feels hot, come back."

John's arm eventually healed but the story was told many times. It made Maggie fearful of telling Da about her knee.

Bridgie noticed Maggie limping as she left for school. "What's happened to your foot? Are your shoes too tight?"

"It's not me foot. It's me knee, but don't tell Da."

Bridgie gave Maggie a nod. She knew her eleven-year-old sister was not afraid of Da. She was trying to protect him from one more worry. The children knew instinctively how hard Bridget's death had impacted their father. They saw him struggle everyday to keep them fed, clothed and safe. He helped with schoolwork, butchered chickens, set curfews for Patrick and took them to Church on Sundays, all while running his forge. They saw Mollie's letters arrive with money and they realized her contributions helped to keep the family intact.

After school on Monday, Da announced that there was a new doctor at the surgery; the "contrary one" had relocated. "After dinner, Maggie, we will go and check your knee."

The new doctor never mentioned a fee. He examined Maggie and recommended she visit the doctor at Cavan Hospital. "I can give her a treatment, but they can better assess the injury by using a series of weights that I don't have available.

Da smiled at Maggie. "Tomorrow is your lucky day, no school. We'll go to Cavan Hospital as this doctor suggests."

Two visits later, it was recommended they visit Dublin Hospital. Da, however, had too many negative feelings about Dublin Hospital. His trips to the hospital with Bridget kept surfacing in his mind. He was silent all the way back to the cottage. He decided to go back to the young doctor in the surgery and ask his opinion. Then I will ask Bridget's best friend. I need a woman's opinion.

Johnny doubled up his work at the forge on Monday and Tuesday. They left for Dublin on Wednesday. He saw the concern in Maggie's eyes.

"We will have a wonderful ride on the train and wait till you see all the excitement in Dublin." But, even as he spoke, the fear inside him made his stomach queasy.

The x-ray results were not good. There was a diagonal crack in Maggie's kneecap. The doctors recommended surgery to remove her kneecap, which meant Maggie would never be able to bend her knee again. She would also need to remain in the children's wing, after surgery, for several months of therapy.

Johnny was upset with the news. How could he leave his little girl in Dublin? Poor child had just lost her mother. He said in a low voice, "we're going home."

Da was relieved that all was well in the cottage when they returned. His friend, Connor, came by the following day and invited Johnny to a football match in the evening. At the game, Johnny decided to seek Connor's advice, since Connor had six children.

"Do you think I should take her back to Dublin?"

"How long did they say?"

"At least three months for the operation, the healing and the therapy."

"Do they expect that to be a permanent cure?"

"Aye, but she won't be able to bend her knee again."

"Are you fearful?"

"Aye. I am afraid to leave her there. She is so young."

"Aye, but that's the point. She is so young. She needs her leg for the rest of her life. Whatever you decide Johnny, don't let it be your fear of leaving, that gets in the way."

Bridgie was packing a case for Maggie to take with her to the hospital when Maggie started to cry.

"What's wrong Maggie?"

"I don't want to go to Dublin Hospital."

"But the doctors will fix your knee and then you'll come back home to us. The time will go quickly and Da said I could visit you there."

"But when I come home, will I die like Mam?"

Bridgie pulled Maggie tight, smoothed the child's hair with one hand and rubbed her back with the other. The emotion of the moment prevented her from speaking. She kept soothing her little sister. Finally, Bridgie spoke.

"I miss Mam too and it's alright to cry. But, she would want you to go to the hospital and get better, Maggie. Mam had something very different than you. Mam understood that there was no treatment for her. So, she came home to be with us before she died. You will not die, Maggie. Your leg will heal and we'll run across the field again. And if you need help, I'll be here, and Da, and Patrick, and all of us. Look how well John's arm has healed. You will heal too. I will ask Da if I can go with the two of you to Dublin. Would you like that?"

"Aye. Come with me," said Maggie in a pleading voice.

The leaving in Dublin was painful for all three. Bridgie promised to write and visit when she could. Da promised he would be back on Sunday.

Once they were seated on the train, Bridgie leaned her head on Da's shoulder. He spoke to her in a choked voice, "Bridgie, you were wonderful with Maggie." Bridgie smiled and promptly fell asleep.

Ballygwen Cottage

The sons came to the table together to speak to their parents. Joan and Thomas were unprepared for the stunning news. Thomas and Paddy were both leaving for England. Paddy would leave in two weeks and Thomas in a month.

Joan couldn't speak. She sat at the table feeling numb. Their father, Thomas, also was silent. The boys expected the news to be difficult, but they never anticipated silence.

Dublin Hospital

Maggie's stay at the Children's Hospital lengthened from three months to two years. She resided in the children's wing where she attended school everyday and worked on her physical therapy. But she missed the cottage.

Da worked out a routine to visit Maggie once or twice a month. He bicycled the two miles to Cavan Town on Sundays. Once there, he visited another blacksmith who stored the bicycle in his shed for the day. Then he rode the train to Dublin. If he had the money for two tickets, he would take one of the younger children with him to visit with Maggie.

Maggie's doctor surprised her one day when he completed his exam and said, "Young lady, you can go home now." The nurse at his side followed with "I will write to your father and have him meet your train."

Maggie was going home! She gathered her meager belongings, said lengthy farewells to her classmates and made promises to write to each and every one. Then with her shoulders back and head high, she walked out the door of Dublin Hospital without a cane.

Her favorite nurse walked her to the nearby train station, purchased a ticket and settled Maggie on board. Maggie's excitement unsuccessfully tried to hurry the train along.

She hoped Da brought the cart and the others with him to meet the train. She hadn't seen little Barney, Patrick or John since she had left home. What will I do first when I arrive home? Bridgie will probably make tea for all of us. That will be wonderful, tea with everyone in the kitchen. Then, I will run to the well, and jump in a haystack. I hope the dogs and the donkey remember me.

While Maggie busied herself with pleasant thoughts, the daylight turned to dusk and it was dark when the train arrived into Cavan Town. The conductor carried Maggie's bag and assisted her down the train steps to the platform.

"Who is meeting you, Miss?"

"Me Da is coming."

"I don't see anyone here."

"Oh, maybe he is late, but he will be here."

"Good night then. I must get back on board."

The train pulled out and Maggie looked around in the darkness. No Da.

Maggie walked to the road that entered the station area and looked into the distance. No sign of a cart approaching. A husband and wife standing nearby had hired a car to take them home. The husband loaded the luggage and the wife spoke to Maggie.

"We are going to Ballinagh. Can we give you a ride?" she asked kindly.

"I am going to Clareboy. I don't know what to do. Me Da is always on time but there is no sign of him."

"You can ride with us, it is the same road. If we meet your Da, we can stop. I don't think you should stay here alone, in the dark."

"Thank you. I will ride with you."

Maggie had never ridden in such luxury before; this was her first time in an automobile. She had her best manners. As the car approached the village of Ballinagh and there was still no sign of Da, the husband asked the driver how much would he charge to drive Maggie to Clareboy after he dropped them at Ballinagh.

"That would be one pound ten pence, sir."

"That settles it then. Take the young lady to Clareboy after you drop us. I will give you the fare."

"Yes, sir."

Maggie asked them for their names so she could write a proper thank you once home. She thanked them profusely and said that Da would repay them the one pound ten pence.

"I won't hear of it," said the husband.

"I am pleased we met and good luck," said the wife. They both climbed out of the car.

The driver was silent once the adults were gone. Maggie rode in the back seat. When she realized the driver had missed the road to Clareboy, she spoke up.

"Isn't that the road to Clareboy?" The driver looked at her in the rear view mirror.

"I'm dropping you in Kilnaleck. It's on me way."

"But the man paid you to take me to Clareboy."

"Well, things are not always as we planned. For example, where is your Da? I'm dropping you in Kilnaleck."

The driver pulled up on the main street, took Maggie's

case from the boot of the car, then opened her door and commanded, "Out."

Maggie stood in the center of the dark street. She was confused. Whatever could have happened to Da? It was now almost midnight and all the windows in the town were dark. Mollie decided she had to walk the three miles to home. She lifted the case and started down the road.

The darkness made her nervous. She hadn't been on her own since before she went to the hospital. She tried to think happy thoughts and walk in the middle of the road, away from any small animals hiding in the bushes. She listened attentively for any signs of danger. Her leg had plenty of physical therapy, but it did not prepare her for this long trek.

At the end of the first mile, she was exhausted. She sat down on her case for a rest. She massaged her weak leg and decided she would take the shortcut across the fields. It would be scary crossing the fields at night, but it was so much shorter. Suddenly, she had an idea, hide the case in some bushes. She could retrieve it tomorrow with Patrick or John. The case was slowing her down and adding fatigue to her leg. Her eyes were adjusting to the darkness now and she spotted a hollow under a dead tree stump. Just the kind of hiding place she needed. She tucked the suitcase in carefully and covered the opening with some leaves. Satisfied that it was safe, she cut across the fields.

In the darkness, she could see the outline of the cottage up ahead. There was no light within. She wondered if they were out searching for her. Maybe I should have stayed on the road. If they were searching, I would never be found in the fields.

As she approached the cottage, there was no sound. She tried the door handle but it was bolted. Should I sleep in the barn? She decided to bang on the door. Inside, she heard the younger children rustle in their beds and finally, Da's voice called out, "Who goes there?"

There were all sorts of commotion and excitement as the door opened and Maggie stepped into the kitchen.

Maggie standing behind Dodie and Barney Lynch

"Maggie, did you run away from the hospital?"asked Da.

"Didn't you get the nurse's letter?"

"No, there was no letter."

"The nurse wrote that I was coming home and asked you to meet the train." Then Maggie related her experience with the driver and her struggle to cut across the fields.

The other children were quiet and hanging on every word.

"You wouldn't be playing a trick on me now, would you?"

"No, Da. It's true."

"Me last visit to Dublin, there wasn't a word about you coming home soon. What changed, I wonder?"

"It was very sudden. One day the doctor came to give me an exam, and he said I could leave and then the nurse said she would write to you."

Suddenly, father started to laugh while he pulled Maggie close and hugged her. "You are a tough one, little lady. I hope the letter arrives, I don't want to have to take you back to Dublin."

"Don't take her back, Da. Let her stay. Please," cried Dodie. "She can sleep with me, like we did before she went away. There's plenty of room. I want her to stay."

Da smiled at Dodie. "She is stayin' now stop yer fussin'. I think this calls for a cup of tea, in spite of the fact that it's the middle of the night."

Two days went by and there was still no letter. Da was beginning to wonder if his suspicions were correct. Did Maggie run away from the hospital? Wouldn't they have given a father some warning if they were planning to release her after such a long stay? He had to admit, he was thrilled to see her around the cottage again. No matter that there were six others, if one of your ducklings is missing, you feel it. And Dodie was beside herself with joy to have Maggie home again. Only two years younger, Dodie had missed Maggie the most. When I go to town on Saturday, I will ring the hospital office and see what they say about Maggie. As it turned out, he did not have to ring, the nurse's letter arrived on Friday, a week late.

Maggie meantime, was delighted to be at home. She ran to the well as she had proposed, jumped in the haystack and rode the donkey. She and Dodie were inseparable. For the first time that Maggie could remember, Barney joined them; two years before he was only a toddler.

What amazed Maggie was the size of her three brothers. Patrick was wider, more like a man now, while John and Larry matched Patrick in height. So much had occurred while she was away. She wrapped her arms around herself and wriggled with delight. "I'm so happy to be home."

Ballygwen
Spring

It was early spring and the rainy season. The winter winds had done their damage to the roof and the last rain had caused a leak in the thatch over the kitchen table. Thomas decided that he had procrastinated far too long and today was the day to fix the roof. He borrowed a ladder and climbed up to determine how much of an area he would have to replace.

It didn't take long to determine that he needed to replace the entire northwest corner of the roof, more than he wanted to do. In spite of the size of the patch, he assembled the materials and proceeded to climb back onto the roof. The task was moving along easy enough, but the weather started to change and a strong wind began to blow in from the ocean.

A neighbor passing by called out, "Thomas, come down from there. The wind is picking up and you will be blown off."

"It will take a hell of a wind to blow me off this roof." And for effect, Thomas stood and stretched out his arms indicating the expanse of the roof.

"Ah, you old-timers are tough lads, sure enough, but I am not pleased to see you up there today. Come down and tomorrow I will lend you a hand. Sure, we'll finish it together in no time."

Joan heard the conversation and came out to see what was happening. She agreed with the neighbor man but decided to hold her opinion and not challenge Thomas.

Realizing his words were having no effect, the neighbor left and returned to his own work. Around noon, Joan came outside again and called for Thomas to come down and into the cottage for his midday meal.

"Don't have much more to go now. Hold the meal a little longer."

Joan was thinking to herself how much longer it took both of them to do their chores now. Thomas was seventy-six and she was seventy-eight. Sure, Thomas could have fixed that thatch in thirty minutes when he was young. The aches and the bones do slow us down nowadays. Both of them had slowed considerably after the letter arrived six months earlier. Bill Broderick, Mary Cecilia's husband, died suddenly in New York, leaving Mary alone to raise their six children. The letter containing the news was worn from the many times it was handled. Thomas cried and often lamented, "Lord, it should have been me." He had never forgiven himself for Mary Cecilia's departure and now, she had a burden and he couldn't help. The distance was a curse. Her thoughts were interrupted with the sound of a loud thud. Thomas was blown off the roof.

Thomas had been kneeling on his right knee, almost finished with the thatch, when a huge gust of wind knocked him off balance and he tumbled to the ground. He was conscious, but unable to get on his feet. The neighbors heard the commotion and came running to help. Several of the men carried Thomas into the cottage and placed him on his bed. The doctor came, determined nothing was broken but bed rest was needed.

Thomas eventually recovered from his fall, but he was never the same. His strength was gone, but more than that, his will to be strong was gone. Thomas died in the cottage on the 7th of April.

"Our Father, who art in heaven, hallowed be they name . . ." The assembled crowd prayed the rosary. Afterwards, there were the stories and the whiskey. One neighbor insisted she heard the Banshee wail the mornin' of the fall. "I was alone in me kitchen when I heard the wailing and the crying. I thought to me self, Mother of God, that's the Banshee. Who is dead this day? And wasn't it only a few hours later I heard the terrible news of the fall. 'Tis a terror, I do say."

The neighbors came from all around the area; Brandon, Cloghane, Lis and Teer. Thomas was well liked and it showed with the number of people visiting.

Joan was not well and the shock of Thomas passing left her disoriented. She was not able to follow the casket to the Cloghane Chapel. Instead, her sister Nan stayed behind with her, made tea and together the sisters prayed the rosary for the repose of his soul. Joan's faith was strong and she believed the angels had already taken Thomas to his heavenly reward. After the funeral, several friends stopped back to the cottage to tell Joan the details of the funeral Mass and the words spoken by Fr. Sean.

The days after the funeral passed slowly. Joan was alone now; the children and grandchildren beyond her reach. She sat by the fire, ate her porridge and drank some tea. The days were endless. She reminisced about her days in Holyoke, how she fell in love with Thomas on the mountain in Lis. She wondered if she was the blame for all her children leaving. Wasn't she the one who sent a crying Mary Cecilia to the States? She always believed it was the fault of Thomas, but now she wasn't so sure.

She thought about how different things might have been if she stayed in Holyoke. The comfort of central heat would be a blessing for these old bones. Sometimes, Holyoke seemed like a distant dream, as if it had never been reality.

There was one source of enjoyment in her daily routine. His name was Johnny, the postman. Johnny Lenihan was her nephew, one of Mane's sons. He passed her cottage everyday on his mail route and everyday he brought cheer to her empty hours.

"How are ye today, Auntie Joan. Have ye a smile for me?"

"Always a smile for you, Johnny, lad."

"Get the tea going, woman. I'll fill your water buckets at the well and be back in a flash."

Johnny never missed a day, even on Sundays, when the mail was not delivered, he stopped by the cottage. He brought her milk from the shop, some homemade bread from his wife, Peg and sometimes, a letter from one of her children.

"Johnny, can you give a message to Brian the carpenter for me? Tell him I need to see him as soon as possible. Tomorrow, if he can come."

"What would ye be needing Brian for? I can fix that broken shelf for you."

"No, no. I am enough of a bother to you. Tell Brian, I need him here and I have the money to pay him for his work. That should encourage him."

Brian came to visit Joan on Sunday, after Mass.

"I got your message. What are you needing Joan?"

"I need you to measure me, for my coffin."

"Well, I can do that but surely, you won't be needing it soon."

"I need to know that things are in order. It gives me peace of mind. Here is the money and thank you for responding so quickly to my message. Now that our business is done, would you like a cup of tea?"

"Aye, I would."

On Monday, Johnny the postman whistled as he came down the lane. Joan was feeling stronger today after her visit with Brian the carpenter. She was prepared now.

"A letter from England, Joan."

"Oh, thank goodness, a letter." She opened it quickly and began to read. "It's from Thomas. He is coming to visit me in July with his wife and two children. Thank you Jesus, Mary and Joseph, I can't wait to see them."

"Ah, that is indeed good news. Can I whitewash the kitchen for you? Before they come?"

Joan was counting the days to July. It gave her joy to anticipate the homecoming. "Oh, to see my lovely grandchildren." Thomas and Mary had a daughter, Eileen, and a son, Michael. Thomas had respected the tradition and so the chain of names, Thomas had Michael and Michael had Thomas, was continued.

While Joan was distracted with counting the days and making her plans for July, her health deteriorated. Thomas and his family arrived three days before Joan's death. It was peaceful for Joan with her family surrounding her. She thanked God that they were here, that she was not alone, that she saw the golden curls on her granddaughter and the impish smile of her grandson. She believed the Lord had allowed her three more days just to see them. Joan died on the 2nd of August, three months after her husband, Thomas.

Michael heard the news that both his parents were gone. He was sorry that he had never made it back to visit before he lost them, but was consoled with having helped them out these last few years. The pain of grieving was still in his heart when a letter arrived from his brother Paddy.

18 Noel Road
Edgbaston
Birmingham 16 England
7 September

Dear Brother,
It's about time I wrote to you. But in times like this we look

forward for consolation towards one another. How are you and your family getting on? I hope ye are all well and happy. Well Michael, Father and Mother are gone now. That only leaves the few of us in this ugly world. No matter how old they were, we always miss them when they are gone, as they were the stock. The old home of which we used often think about. Never mind, everything must have an end.

Thomas was home when Mother died and he said she was resigned to it as she was very lonely after Father and living on her own was not the thing. I was home to see them last summer. It is just a year ago now. They looked terrible old and feeble. Father was very bad on the feet and his head used to play him up as well. I guessed he would only live about seven to nine months. Mother was hardy that time, very worn on the face and thin but still kept the old spirit up and was very cheerful. Considering, they were both very happy and cheerful. A lot of the old neighbors used to come in and chat with them and the days used seem to slip away fast enough. The old house, the old garden and concerns are still the same as when you left. I spent a month there. I was sorry when I was coming away. They were very lonely after us. I intended going again next year but no interest now.

Well Michael, I suppose things over there in the USA is still not all sunshine too. It must be very similar to this country, watching the clock, rush and worry. How is Mary Cecilia? Tell her to write or I'll knock her block off when I see her. I heard some wrinkle that her husband died. I hope not, as I would be so sorry.

I have four children now, Michael. All girls. They are proper little beauties. The baby is only four months old, Bernadette Geraldine, as cute as you like. My wife had to have an operation to have her and she was very bad. I suppose you know we had one little boy and he died at birth. I have Mary Cecilia 8 years, Joan Veronica 6 years, Kathleen Anne 4 years and the baby, as I stated.

Well, I must now finish, as I have no more to say. Hoping to hear from you soon. The Best of Luck and love from Pat, wife and family to you, your wife and your family.

P.S. Please write soon as I am dying to hear from ye.

Late one night, after work, Michael sat at the kitchen table to pen his response to Paddy. He took his time with it, wanting to choose the right words to tell him that indeed, Mary's husband had died. But his letter arrived too late.

Paddy died suddenly on the 9th of December, only three months after writing to Michael. In one year, the Finn family had lost Mother, Father, Paddy and Bill Broderick.

There were now ten grandchildren without a father.

New York
Summer 1934

Patrick was short of breath, tired, and barely able to drag his body to work. On his day off, all he wanted to do was sleep and that was out of character. It was over dinner one evening that Mary Galligan prompted him to see the doctor.

"Patrick, you're not yourself these days. You've hardly got an appetite and your color is like snow. I don't like it. Don't like it at all. You're to see the doctor this week. I won't hear another word about it."

Mary's husband, Matty, and her two children listened without saying a word. It wasn't often they heard Mary speak with such authority in her voice and they recognized it as a time to agree with her. Patrick looked across the table to Matty for support, forcing a response from the other adult male in the room.

"Yes, I agree, you are not looking well. I have the telephone number of a good doctor on East 87th Street. I will give it to you later and you can ring his office tomorrow." Realizing Patrick still had not agreed to go, he continued, "I can go with you, if you plan for the late afternoon."

"Sure it's no bother to you Matty, I can find the way over there. Just give me the number."

The doctor's office was only four subway stops from Patrick's

Post Office. He phoned ahead and the receptionist told him he could come that same day. He exited the subway station at the East 86th Street station and walked the one block north to the office. There were several other patients waiting when he arrived, but the line moved quickly.

Dr. McGrath was about forty-five years of age, with a quick smile and a pleasant demeanor. He sensed that his new patient was extremely nervous, so he extended his hand to Patrick and tried to put the nervous man at ease with some chatter.

"So are you the man responsible for my excellent mail delivery?"

"If it is excellent service, I am indeed the one responsible," joked Patrick in response.

"Well, let me have a look at you, Mr. Mailman. We need to keep men like you moving at your best."

The exam took almost an hour with Dr. McGrath checking some responses twice and asking Patrick to give him some blood and saliva samples. He also ordered a chest x-ray and sent Patrick to the hospital across the street for this. He directed Patrick to wait for the film and bring it back to him as soon as it was completed. When Patrick returned in two hours with the x-ray film, the office was empty.

Dr. McGrath called him into the examination room and placed the film over the light tray. He came right to the point.

"I've some serious news for you Patrick. Your x-ray and shortness of breath indicates that you have contracted tuberculosis. I will not know what stage until your blood samples are returned from the lab. In the meantime, we will start treatment and you must follow my directions exactly. Hopefully, we have caught it in an early stage and medication will keep it under control. If it has progressed, you will have to report to a sanatorium for quarantine. I am sorry to give you this bad news."

Patrick asked if there could be some mistake. Was Dr. McGrath absolutely sure about the results? He was tired but he didn't feel sick enough to have TB. There must be some mistake.

"I'm sorry Patrick, but there is no mistake. Now, tell me, who do you live with?"

Patrick told him about Mary and Matty and the two children.

"They will all have to come here for an exam," ordered Dr. McGrath. TB is highly contagious and you must protect your family. Tell them to come as soon as possible."

As Patrick rode the subway home to the Galligan household he thought about the words he would use to tell Matty and Mary. The last thing he wanted was to bring TB to them or God forbid, to the children. He decided to be direct and stress the importance of immediate care.

He climbed the stairs to the fourth floor. When he entered, he was pleased that only Mary and Matty were at home.

"I need to speak to you both."

"What's wrong, Patrick?" questioned Matty.

"Dr. McGrath says its TB. No mistake about it."

"Oh, no."

"He will know in a few days how serious it is when the blood work is finished."

"Is there medicine for it?"

"Yes, he gave me some tablets."

"Can you go to work?"

"I can go to work if I feel well enough. At least until the tests are back. If the test is not good, I'll need a TB hospital or a rest home." He stopped talking allowing all he had said to be absorbed. No one spoke for several minutes. "The important part for you and the children is that Dr. McGrath wants to see all of you, right away. He wants to give you an exam because you've been exposed, especially the children. I told him you both work but you'll have to take off. You need to see him tomorrow."

In the days that followed, Patrick continued working, the Galligan family got their exams and every afternoon Pat telephoned Dr. McGrath's office to see if his results had arrived. On the ninth day, the receptionist told him to come in that afternoon after work.

"Hello Patrick. How have you been feeling with the tablets I gave you?"

"A little better. I can get up easier in the morning but in an hour or two, I'm the same."

"The Galligans have a fine family. How are they feeling these days?"

"They appear to be fine. Thank you for taking care of them. I couldn't deal with them getting sick because of me."

"Hopefully, we've caught this in time and the treatments will work. You must take your tablets religiously and never miss your weekly visit. Don't give this a chance to get ahead of us."

Six weeks passed with Patrick following the routine. At the Galligan house he used only one set of dishes, washed them himself and kept them in his room. He got more rest and in general, tried not to over exert his lungs. He went to Dr. McGrath's office for his weekly exam. It was part of his routine now so he was taken by surprise when the Doctor asked him to sit down.

"I've some bad news for you, Patrick. Your lungs have stopped responding. That means you will be highly contagious again. You will need to go to a sanitarium. Soon."

"You mean just pack up and leave? Leave my job? Where will I go?"

"I have several good places I can recommend. You could choose from my list."

"What will it cost? And how can I pay for the treatments if I'm not working?"

"Don't panic, I realize this is difficult. My receptionist and I will help you get it organized. I see from your file that you are a veteran of World War I. We will apply to the Veterans Administration first, since you are entitled to benefits.

It took almost two weeks to arrange for Patrick's bed in the VA hospital at Tupper Lake. It was located in upstate New York where the country air was helpful for healing.

It was difficult to say goodbye to his niece, Mollie, to Mary and Matty and the children. They were his New York family.

"Not to worry Patrick, we'll be writing to you every week

and when we're allowed, we'll be on the train to visit," assured Mary.

"Can we, Mom? Can we take the train to see Patrick? That would be great!" pleaded Matty Junior.

"Yes, we will."

Little Rosemary handed Patrick a sheet of paper. "I made you a drawing, Patrick. It's for your new room."

"It's lovely. I will post it where everyone can see it," and he bent to hug her.

Mollie spoke next. "If you need anything, just write. I'll see to it."

Tupper Lake
September 1934

Patrick arrived at Tupper Lake in mid-September. As he stepped from the train, the fall air touching his cheeks was brisk and invigorating. The trees had changed their leaves to vibrant colors of red, orange and yellow. The sky was blue and the abundance of chirping birds gave the entire scene an aura of peacefulness. It reminded him of the farm in Ireland and lifted his spirits. He had dreaded coming to this place but once here, he found himself responding to the serenity. Perhaps I did need a rest from the city.

"Patrick Lynch?" a stranger asked him.

"Yes."

"I am the VA driver. Come with me to the car. I will carry your case."

When Patrick first arrived at Tupper Lake, he was assigned to a room with three other men. Two of the men, Walter and Victor, had been there a month before Pat arrived while the third man, nicknamed Sarge, arrived only a day before. Walter and Victor enjoyed showing Sarge and Pat "the ropes." They went to meals together in the mess hall and pointed out the best desserts. They played cards in the rec room and spent hours sharing war stories. They had all served in the "Great

War." Wally showed the most damage, an amputated leg and a twitch in his left eye. The others hid their scars inside.

Sarge was the biggest of the men. He stood six feet four inches tall and weighed about three hundred pounds. He enjoyed giving Pat a bear hug and lifting him high off the floor. Pat didn't mind, it was all part of the new camaraderie they were sharing. Sarge would direct Pat in the cafeteria. "Eat more food, soldier. You need to put more meat on them bones, you're too thin."

The foursome spoke very little of the TB that had brought them together. Once, when Walter was in a dark mood, he lectured the others.

"Do you guys know Smitty, down the hall from us? Well, he's being moved to the second floor. I just found out. That means he is worse. Everyone starts on the third floor. If you improve, you go home. If you deteriorate, you go to two. Second floor guys have more medication and more restrictions. The first floor is for the end. More nurses and you're in bed all the time. Smitty is upset. He just got the word and he's moving this morning. I saw him packing up his duffel bag."

No one spoke. They didn't question Walter, they believed him. They had been behaving as if they were at a resort, with not a care in the world. There was an unspoken code that if you didn't talk about it, it would go away. Smitty moving to the second floor was like hitting a brick wall. There it was, large, real and probably inevitable for all of them. It was just a matter of time. They sat in silence.

The mood was broken when a nurse named Suzie entered the rec room.

"Hey guys. We're having a horse race tournament this afternoon. You four want to be a team? Give yourselves a team name and meet me here at fifteen hundred hours."

All the guys liked Suzie. She was a good sport, quick with the comebacks and showed concern for each of "her guys," as she called her assigned section of the third floor. It sure helped that she was attractive. A good figure, long brunette hair tied back loosely with a ribbon, great smile and large green eyes completed the package. Wally had a huge crush on Suzie.

Victor answered first. "What's in it for the winners? Can we play for cigarettes?"

Suzie gave him a frown. Cigarettes were forbidden at Tupper Lake and so was alcohol. Visitors had to leave their bags in lockers to ensure no one broke the rules.

"Sure, I'll pick up a pack of Camels when I go to town."

They all laughed. Victor continued. "As long as you are going shopping, how about four bottles of beer to finish the job?"

Suzie waved her hand at them, rolled her eyes and continued out the door, calling over her shoulder, "Fifteen hundred hours, be there."

Wally was the first to be moved to the second floor. He remained strong when he got the news. Told everyone he was gonna be the first to leave two and come back to join them on three. They toasted his idea with glasses of orange juice and made a date for a reunion at McSorley's Bar in Manhattan, one-year from today.

Patrick received letters every week as Mary Galligan had promised. She kept him up to date on the local gossip and what was happening at school with the children. Matty Jr. was still waiting for Patrick to get the doctors approval for visitors, so they could ride the train to Tupper Lake. Mollie was also faithful about writing. In her last letter she told him all about Michael.

Patrick moved to the second floor one month after his arrival. He had anticipated the move when his breathing started to have a wheezing sound. He had heard that same sound from Wally and he knew.

The second floor was quieter than the third. There were mandatory nap times during the day and Patrick was just as pleased. He was tired. There was more medication and daily visits from the chaplain.

Fr. Serra wore his military uniform on his rounds. He

stopped at each bedside getting to know the soldiers' names and passed out chocolate bars, chewing gum, mints and words of encouragement. If asked, he wrote letters for those needing assistance. Patrick noticed that Fr. Serra spent more time than usual with the guys who were soon moved to the first floor. Patrick wondered if the nurses told him who was next to move or if the priest sensed it on his own. Patrick heard that Victor died in his sleep on the third floor. Then Wally moved to one and passed in three days. Now there was only Sarge, still on three and Patrick on two.

"Newspapers, books, magazines" called out the man pushing the reading cart through the ward. Pat looked up, the voice sounded familiar. It was Sarge.

"What the hell are you doing here?" laughed Patrick as he slapped the big man on his back.

"Came to see if you gained any weight, you little runt," answered Sarge.

"You're not supposed to be down here Sarge. You know this floor is quarantined."

"Had to come and see my buddy. I got this orderly to loan me his cart for an hour. That's how I was able to sneak in."

"Great to see you." They talked for half an hour when Patrick noticed the nurse coming for medication rounds.

"You better get, while you can," suggested Patrick.

"See ya buddy. Don't forget McSorley's"

"See ya there, Sarge." The cart wheeled out of the ward in the opposite direction of the nurse.

Patrick started to see more of Fr. Serra and he knew.

New York City
November 1934

Mollie got a message at work from Fr. Serra. He wanted Mollie to come to Tupper Lake as soon as possible, Patrick was dying. It was Tuesday at noon when Mollie got the message. She left work and headed to Grand Central Station for the next train to Tupper Lake. She called from a payphone at the station and left messages at work for Aunt Mary and another for Michael. Then she called Tupper Lake leaving a message for Fr. Serra that her train would arrive at six in the morning. To help pass the time, she bought a cup of tea and a sandwich, even though she wasn't hungry. She carefully wrapped the half of sandwich remaining and placed it in her purse for later.

The train departed on time. It was Tuesday evening, November seventh, with the temperature well below freezing and the night-lights of the city already glowing. Mollie found a comfortable seat and the conductor came by to punch her ticket. He read her destination.

"Tupper Lake, you change trains at the Newburgh station. About three hours from here. I'll remind you."

She had a newspaper to read but within half an hour, the rocking of the train and the warmth of the compartment lulled her to sleep. Mollie woke with a startle when the conductor touched her shoulder.

"Newburgh Station coming up in ten minutes."

She rubbed her eyes, visited the ladies room and prepared to disembark.

When Mollie stepped out of the train onto the station, it had started to snow. She hustled into the country style ticket office with the other transfer passengers. A conductor announced that the Tupper Lake train was delayed.

The train arrived an hour late. By now it was snowing heavily and the temperature had dropped another five degrees. The little group boarded the train and settled in. It didn't take long to realize there was no heat on this train and the wind whistled through a crack in the glass. Mollie pulled her coat closer, turned up the collar and put on her gloves. The lights on this train flashed on and off at irregular intervals making it impossible to read. It was going to be a long night.

Unable to sleep, Mollie's thoughts were of Uncle Pat. She owed him so much. He had brought her to this country, to a new life. Although she had tried to repay her fare, he had not accepted it. He told her to send it home to Clareboy; it was needed there. He was always a little awkward around her but she knew, in his own way, he cared about her, loved her. They only had each other in New York and now she was losing him. When he left for Tupper Lake she naively believed he would recover and return to the city. Perhaps it was his nonchalant attitude when leaving that had disarmed her, or was she too wrapped up with her own life to see the danger ahead? Looking back, she realized it had been his deliberate plan not to worry her. Now it was too late. She hoped that he would not die alone, that she would get to him in time with words that would bring comfort.

Mollie's teeth began to chatter from the cold. She stood up and stomped her feet to get the circulation going again. She looked out the window at the accumulating snowfall then looked down at her black leather pumps. She had bought them last payday but she knew they would be useless in this blizzard.

"Tupper Lake, next stop."

Mollie stepped off the train and into the blizzard. The wind was swirling the snow, making it difficult to see and the drifts completely covered her shoes, her ankles, and the calf of her leg. Her city outfit was inadequate for this winter blast. She took only three steps forward, just enough to move away from the train that would soon pull out. She stood frozen in that spot, squinting her eyes in an attempt to see which direction to the car park. Fr. Serra was to meet her there but now it was buried beneath the snow. She shifted her overnight case from one numb hand to the other and saw headlights flashing through the snow. It was a truck moving slowly in the direction of the platform. A man jumped out of the truck dressed in a khaki green army overcoat; black high laced military boots and an officer's hat. He called out in the semi-darkness, "Miss Lynch?"

She waved her hand in response and struggled to walk towards the truck.

She was expecting Fr. Serra, a priest with a white collar and black suit but he must have sent someone else to pick her up. Since he knew her name, she felt safe going with this soldier.

Once she got close enough, the soldier extended his hand and took her suitcase.

"I'm Fr. Serra. Thank you for coming so quickly and braving this blizzard. You must be frozen."

"It wasn't snowing when I left Manhattan, so I am not dressed for this storm."

"Did you get any sleep on the train?"

"A little."

"I am going to take you to Rosemarie's home. She works at the hospital and helps out when families come to visit. You can't stay at the hospital or eat there because of the TB. Rosemarie will have some dry clothes for you, a pair of boots and a hot breakfast. It's 6 am now, you can sleep for a few hours and I'll return for you at ten and take you to see Pat."

"I appreciate all your efforts to help me and Uncle Pat."

"He has been strong through this ordeal. He told me all about your parents and the forge and your coming to the States. He said you're wonderful, a good worker, kind, honest and thoughtful."

Mollie felt her face flush with embarrassment. This stranger knew so much about her and her family. He continued talking as if it were important to tell her everything. The truck continued slowly through the snow.

"Patrick told me he never had a close woman relative, no sisters, his mother died when he was an infant, so he wasn't sure how to treat you. I think he regrets not giving you more attention."

"He was always good to me. The first time he visited us in Clareboy, I was fourteen and he's been a part of my life ever since."

"He only has a short time left. Anything you need to say should be said today."

Fr. Serra pulled the truck into the driveway of a modest

sized house on the main road. He helped her out and half carried her through the drifts to the back door. Rosemarie hustled them into the kitchen, took Mollie's wet coat, gave her warm slippers and wrapped a blanket around her. She guided Mollie to a chair in front of her living room fireplace and put a mug of hot coffee into her hands.

"What an unexpected blizzard! You were lucky the train tracks remained open. Sometimes, when the snow is unexpected, like today, the trains get stalled and the passengers are stranded. Are you warming up?"

"Yes, thank you so much, Rosemarie, I was frozen."

Fr. Serra spoke next. "I've got to be going. I have morning mass at the hospital. I'll be back for Miss Lynch at ten."

"Call me Mollie."

Fr. Serra and Mollie entered the hospital together through the side door. They walked down a long corridor with rooms to the right and left. They passed several nurses and two patients sitting in wheelchairs who greeted Fr. Serra. They continued to the end of the hall and turned left. Fr. Serra stopped outside the second door.

He turned to Mollie. "Do you want me to go in with you?"

"Yes, please."

Patrick was just finishing a few tablespoons of soup. The nurse feeding him was preparing to remove the tray when they entered. Patrick's face broke into a broad smile when he saw Mollie. She gave him a hug and a kiss on his cheek. He was too weak to squeeze back. His voice was hoarse and weak but he made an effort to speak.

"How did you ever find this place, Mollie?"

"Thanks to Fr. Serra I am not a frozen ice stick at the train station. What a huge snowstorm, but I am fine and happy to be here."

Fr. Serra spoke next. "I am going upstairs to check on someone. Be back later."

Patrick and Mollie visited for an hour catching up on news of the family when Patrick put his hand on Mollie's. "I won't be going home to the city, Mollie." She nodded her head. It was too difficult to get words out.

"I want to prepare a will. Can you get some paper?"

Mollie dug around in her purse and came up with two small sheets of paper and a pen. Patrick began to dictate.

"My gold pocket watch and gold watch chain go to my brother Johnny in Clareboy. Also, my good cufflinks, tie tacks and wristwatch. Send him my good suit and bury me in my army uniform. I have some money in the bank, not much left after the crash, but I want you to have fifty dollars. Send the rest to my brother. Give Mary Galligan my other clothing for Matty and twenty-five dollars each for the children. I can't think of anything else now, Mollie. Let me sign what you wrote and then you can add the date. I am very tired."

He scribbled something that resembled his name and fell asleep. Mollie carefully placed the sheets of paper in her purse. She sat by the side of Patrick's bed as he slept. Fr. Serra returned about an hour later. When he saw that Patrick was in a deep sleep, he signaled Mollie to follow him into the hallway.

"He will probably sleep for hours, so you can take a break. I'll take you to Rosemarie's for supper and bring you back again.

"I'd rather stay here. If he should awake, I want to be nearby."

"If you need anything, the nurse at the end of the corridor can help you or she can get a message to me. See you in the morning."

Patrick slept for hours, sometimes moaning, sometimes calling Mollie's name. She stayed at his bedside throughout the night. When Fr. Serra returned at seven in the morning, he found them both asleep. He gently touched Mollie's shoulder.

"Rosemarie packed you a breakfast and hot tea in a thermos. You can eat in the truck. You must be hungry."

"Thank you. I hadn't thought about it, but hot tea sounds wonderful."

After breakfast, she returned to her vigil next to Pat's bed.

At one point, he opened his eyes and unable to speak, he smiled when he saw her.

"I'm right here. I'm not leaving."

Pat nodded, closed his eyes and drifted off to sleep again. The nurse returned to check Patrick and gently told Mollie that he was gone. Fr. Serra came into the room and said the Prayers of the Dead. When finished, he turned to Mollie.

"I can take you to the office. There are papers to sign."

The office clerk asked Mollie for the name of the funeral service director she would be using.

"I don't know. I don't have one."

The clerk gave her a disgusted look. He spoke in a nasty tone. "You can sign here for the routine military funeral and we'll bury him at the Veteran's Cemetery in Tupper Lake. Then you don't have to do anything."

"No, I want to bring him home to the City. I just came to Tupper Lake in a hurry, so I am not prepared."

"Fine. Today is Thursday. We're closed on Monday; it's Veterans Day. Let me know what you're doing." He rudely passed over a card.

Mollie took the first train back to the city and went to Aunt Mary's. Michael met her there. They contacted a recommended funeral director and he arranged for Patrick to be transported back to New York City. He also recommended St. John's Cemetery. They were opening a new section and prices were reasonable. Feeling inadequate and lacking in knowledge of these matters, Mollie rode with the director to the cemetery. He chose an area in the new section and showed it to Mollie. Waving his arms around, he said, "This is a nice spot. It is a grave for three. Maybe someday you'll get married and this will be taken care of for you and your husband. I would recommend buying this plot."

Tuesday morning there was a funeral mass for Patrick at Holy Name Church on 96th Street and Broadway followed by burial at St. John's. It was a military funeral with six soldiers for pallbearers and an American flag draping the casket. Mollie stood tall at the cemetery, aware that her presence represented the entire family. She could anticipate her father's grief caused by the unexpected telegram. The rifle volley made her jump and brought her mind back to the graveside. The bugler started Taps and Mollie's determination to be strong slipped out of her control. She leaned on Michael and Aunt Mary held her around the shoulders. The November wind whipped her legs, chilled her hands and sent shivers to her heart. She was alone now. She bent down, picked up the shell casings, then slowly turned to leave her only family in the earth.

New York City
December 1934

Michael proposed marriage to Mollie. Mollie accepted. It was that simple and inevitable. They had been constant companions for two years and everyone assumed they would marry someday.

Michael was there for Mollie when Patrick died. She loved Michael but experiencing his tenderness and strength throughout the funeral ordeal made her realize what a special person he was in her life.

Michael was excited and started to plan.

"Let's get married for Christmas. Then we could get a place together and have our first Christmas tree. It will be great."

Michael stopped short when Mollie shook her head no.

"I love you Michael but it is too soon. It would be disrespectful to Uncle Pat's memory. I need to wait."

"I'm sorry, I forgot. But that's my girl, always thinking and doing the right thing." He pulled her close and kissed her forehead, her cheek, her neck.

They exchanged rings for Christmas. Michael bought Mollie's engagement ring at Tiffany's on Fifth Avenue. Mollie bought Michael a gold initial ring and had it engraved M.L. to M.F. 12-25-34. They set a wedding date for June.

Mollie Lynch and Michael Finn
Christmas 1935

January 1935

Mollie made plans to travel uptown to the Galligans and meet Aunt Mary while her children were at school. Together, they sorted and packed a trunk of Uncle Pat's belongings from his room. It was one more difficult chore for Mollie. It was not the hard work that she dreaded, she was used to working hard. The difficulty was the emotional attachment to each item and the memories conjured up of a life cut short at forty-six.

The last time Mollie spoke to Patrick at Tupper Lake, there was a sense of something not completed. She reminded him of all that he had done over the years. Even on his deathbed, he was concerned about giving his possessions away to others.

The doorbell interrupted them. It was the man representing the shipping company. Mollie arranged for him to pick up the trunk packed with Pat's belongings. She was shipping it to her father in Clareboy, honoring Patrick's last wishes. The gold pocket watch, chain, cufflinks, and tie tack were enclosed along with the suits, vests, sweaters and other items from Patrick's bureau. In addition, Mollie enclosed gifts for her brothers and sisters. She spent two days shopping and gift wrapping the assortment of clothing, candy and toys. She could visualize the excitement when the trunk was delivered to the cottage and the children gathered around Da for the opening.

Mollie signed the shipping agreement, paid the fees and turned over an envelope containing the key to the trunk along with a completed customs form.

March 1935

Michael was visiting Mollie when the mailman delivered a letter from Clareboy. Excited, Mollie called out, "It's from Da. I'll bet the trunk was delivered. I can't wait to read about his surprise at all the goodies I packed."

But the letter in her hand was a tirade. Father's words were

harsh and irrate. They were written in the heat of anger and
the words jumped off the page causing pain. The color drained
from Mollie's face and she started to shake.

"Mollie, what's wrong?"

She couldn't speak. She handed the letter to Michael. He
read quickly, then started to shout in disbelief.

"The trunk was half empty! No gold pocket watch and
chain, no cuff links, no tie tack, no suit. How could that be?"

They were both silent for a moment. Then Michael started
to pace and curse. "Those sons-of-bitches. They opened the
trunk and stole everything of value. Get your coat Mollie. We're
going over to that thieving shipping office right now. Someone
is going to pay for this."

The man behind the desk listened to the story. He turned
to Mollie and questioned her.

"You gave the pick-up man the keys?"

"Yes. He gave me the marked envelope and I put them
inside. He had me sign the back of the envelope."

"We never take the keys. You're supposed to mail them to
the recipient."

"But he told me that's the process." Her voice was
desperate.

"Let me check the records and see who picked up your
trunk that day." He moved to another desk and began looking
through large diaries with columns of dates and names.

"Says here Thompson picked up that trunk. It figures. He
doesn't work here any longer."

Michael spoke next. "What can we do about this now?"

"I'll have to talk to the boss. I'm really sorry about your
experience. Give me a week, then check back. I'll have an
answer for you."

But Mollie did not have to return to the shipping office
because a notice arrived five days later. Several other customers
reported theft of property in the same manner. The former
employee was arrested and charged. When Michael visited the
next day, Mollie shared the notice with him.

"It is something, but it is not enough. It will never match the memory of the stolen items."

McSorley's Bar, New York City
November 1935

Wearing his old army jacket, Sarge walked into McSorley's bar around noon. He took a seat at the bar and waved to the bartender.

"Give me four shot glasses of whiskey and four beers. Line 'em up right here for me and my friends." Then he removed his jacket, walked to the far wall and hung the jacket on a peg. The bartender looked around, saw no one else, but did as Sarge requested and went back to drying glasses. He noticed that Sarge had finished two of the shots and two of the beers in only a few minutes. He went over and leaned on the bar in front of him.

"Your friends are late?"

"You could say that, I guess." Sarge picked up his third shot glass and knocked it back.

"Whoa slow down, soldier. It's too early in the day."

"I thought your job was to sell this stuff," said Sarge.

"Yeah. Sure. But I got to look out for my customers too. You're a soldier. I was Navy."

Sarge started on beer number three. He was beginning to feel the effects of the liquor. He felt melancholy, started to ramble, and spilled his guts about his friends at Tupper Lake and the reunion.

When Sarge was done with his story, the bartender poured a shot glass for himself and when Sarge picked up his fourth whiskey, they toasted.

Sarge closed his eyes. "To the men of Tupper Lake. May they rest in peace. We will never forget ya."

"Amen," added the bartender. He tipped back his head and threw the shot down his throat in one gulp. Sarge started to sip his last beer.

The bar was suddenly busy with the lunch crowd and the bartender moved to the other end of the bar. When he looked back, Sarge had his head down on his arm, fast asleep. The bartender quietly removed Sarge's glass from the bar, retrieved the army jacket and covered the huge man's shoulders.

New York City
June, 1936

Mollie gave birth to a daughter on June 1, 1936. The baby was two weeks late in arriving and the labor, over thirty hours long, was painful. When Michael was finally permitted to see Mollie, he found her exhausted, but joyful. Michael went to Mollie's bedside and kissed her forehead.

"Michael, have you seen her yet?"

"No, not yet. The nurse told me I could see you and she would bring us the baby."

"Here she is!" called the nurse as she crossed the room and placed the small bundle in Mollie's arms. Michael leaned in close and together they lifted the blanket covering the baby's face.

"She's beautiful," gasped Mollie.

"She's got red hair, like her great grandfather, Mikeen," said Michael in surprise.

"Yes, and look at the long fingers."

All the pain was forgotten as Michael and Mollie prepared the baby for Baptism. They christened her Ann Bridget, after her two grandmothers, Johanna and Bridget. Her godparents were the maid of honor and best man from the wedding, Nellie Cusick and Joe Shea. As luck would have it, Nellie was from Cavan and Joe was from Kerry.

The proud parents planned a house party after the christening. Mollie prepared sandwiches and salads followed with a beautiful cake. Mary and Matty Galligan came along with Rose McConnell and Lena Mullins with her new husband, Tom Healy. Mary Cecilia and her children traveled from Brooklyn with Tom Lorigan, Nellie's future husband. Maureen came with her husband and five-year old daughter.

As the friends began to gather around the table, Nellie let out a sudden small cry. "Oh, no."

"What's wrong?" asked Michael as the others looked on, puzzled.

"I made a terrible mistake. When I gave the priest a contribution for the christening, I must have given him a ten-dollar bill and two singles instead of three singles. I only have a one dollar bill in my purse and it should be a ten."

"And I gave him three dollars because I didn't know you were planning to give him a gift," said Joe, the Godfather.

"And I gave him three dollars," said Michael, "because I didn't know you were planning to give him a gift."

The room erupted with laughter. It was a full five minutes before anyone could speak.

Finally, Michael raised his glass for a toast. "To my wife, Mollie, for the beautiful gift she has given me this day. To the priest, who is the richest man in the parish tonight and to the start of our family and an end to the leaving." The others around the table joined in, holding glasses high, "Slainte."

EPILOGUE

JOHNNY THE BLACKSMITH purchased a farm for his oldest son, Patrick. John, his second son, became the seventh generation blacksmith. He married and raised his family in the Clareboy Cottage.

It was Johnny the blacksmith's intention to secure land for each of his sons but he died unexpectedly in 1937 at age fifty. Barney, his youngest child, was only eleven.

The children from the cottage matured and married producing thirty-one grandchildren for Johnny and Bridget. Patrick and his wife were childless. After their deaths, the farm was sold and the proceeds divided among the surviving nieces and nephews.

Larry was the first of Bridget and Johnny's children to pass. He died in May 1953, at the age of thirty-four, leaving a wife and three children.

Johanna Fitzgerald, her husband Thomas Finn and her son, Patrick, all passed in 1951. Their stories are included here. Mary Cecilia died in 1966 at age sixty-one while Tomasin lived to see three grandchildren and his seventieth birthday in 1984.

Mollie and Michael went on to celebrate sixty-two years of marriage. They had four children, eight grandchildren and five great-grandchildren. Thirty years passed before Mollie and Michael were able to visit home.

Michael died at age ninety in 1997. Mollie is now ninety years old and still strong. Mollie told the stories.

REFERENCES

Family Tree Maker CD. (1999). *International Land Records: Irish Flax Growers, 1796.* Broderbund, The Learning Company.

Flynn, Arthur. (1993). *Book of Kerry: Towns and Villages of the Kingdom.* Dublin, Ireland. Wolfhound Press.

Johnson, Margaret M. (1998, December 16-22). Hunt theWren. *Irish Echo,* pp. 24-25.

McMorran, R. and C. *Cloghane—Brandon Guide.* Available through Cloghane Visitor's Bureau, Co. Kerry.

O'Conghaile, Pol. (2000, Dec. 29-Jan. 11). Echoes of the Millenium, New Year's Eve 1899. *Irish Echo,* pp. 50-51.

BHC Photos purchased through the Ballygwen Heritage Center, Co. Kerry, Ireland.